NEMESIS

NEMESIS

David Pinto

Heliotrope Books
New York

I dedicate this book to my wife, Cindy, and my daughter, Ronit.
With their love and assistance
I am able to pursue my passion for story-telling.

1

"Police station?"

"You must come immediately," Elliot Barrett II implored his lawyer and best friend.

"What in the hell are you doing in a police station?" Ted Lapoltsky shouted.

"Can't talk out here."

"Just tell me if you are in some kind of trouble."

"I think it's a mix up."

"Elliot, listen to me. Don't say anything to the police without me there to represent you. It's very important."

"Just hurry up!" Elliot urged impatiently.

"I'll be there in thirty minutes, you know how Manhattan traffic is. And remember, not a word to anyone."

After getting off the phone, Elliot found himself handcuffed by a police officer and led through long, iron-gated corridors to a small cell with a bunk bed in the right corner. There were no windows, and bright fluorescent lights revealed walls full of scratches and scribbles etched onto the dirty gray surface by its previous prisoners. Elliot's throat was dry and he felt a twisting pain in his stomach. He looked frequently at his watch, as if that would bring Ted faster. His mind raced as he tried to figure out what to tell him.

He must sound convincing, he knew, to himself and to everyone else. He could not afford to ruin his life and reputation as a senior doctor on staff at Sloan-Kettering Cancer Center. He would not be able to face his wife, Ruth, and his two children. He didn't want to compromise his father and mother's status in high-society Boston.

He decided to deny any involvement with Lindsey, the woman he was accused of murdering, beyond his doctor-patient relationship.

Ted looked at the clock. 5:22 P.M. He left his desk in a hurry, told Melissa, his secretary, to cancel all his commitments for the next day and headed down the elevator, not paying any attention to her request for more clarification about where he was going, when he would return.

What a coincidence he thought. *The mouse is in the cage. Who can believe what has happened? I must stay cool and take advantage of the situation. I can't afford to make any mistakes.*

Waiting to catch a taxi, Ted looked at the sky and worried about the threatening dark clouds that might flood the city with rain at any moment and snag traffic even more miserably in the crowded Manhattan streets. He hailed a cab and offered the driver an extra ten dollars to get him downtown as fast as possible. Long ago he had learned that money always paved the way to what he wanted.

Ted rushed through the imposing entry to the police station, through the loud and crowded hallway and headed straight to the station desk. It took a few seconds for the officer in charge to bring up Elliot's record on the computer screen and tell him to wait in a small, private room.

Elliot appeared; he seemed agonized, his eyes lowered. The officer who had escorted him removed his handcuffs. Elliot shook Ted's hand, seeming a little relieved by his presence and fast arrival. He waited until the policeman sat down in the far corner before speaking. "I don't quite understand what is happening."

"Did you say anything to the police?" Ted asked urgently.

"No, you said not to talk—but I have nothing to hide," he said as he nervously rubbed his right eye.

"So what in the hell do they want from you? Is it something to do with taxes? No, that can't be."

"They said I murdered a woman."

"Murder?" Ted shouted, then lowered his voice when he noticed the cop seated in the corner. "What in the hell are you talking about? A mistake with one of your patient's in the operating room?" Ted tried to create surprise in his voice.

"No, not a patient. They said I killed Lindsey Anderson, the daughter of one of my patients."

"Killed a woman? Had you been seeing her?" Ted asked, trying to control his emotions. He wasn't supposed to know anything yet.

"No, no. I told you, Lindsey was the daughter of my patient. I only knew her because of her mother, Margaret."

You son of a gun, Ted was thinking. *I knew you had being seeing her romantically*. He hesitated, taking time to formulate what to say next. "You mean no…"

"The police say they have strong evidence that I murdered her," Elliot said desperately. "They think we were lovers. We weren't."

Ted lowered his voice. "You know Elliot, I have been a criminal defense attorney for a long time. I always tell my clients not to tell me the truth and I manage to get most of them off. But with you I want to hear the truth so I can construct any scenario possible to get you out of this mess. I will never let them…"

"What do you mean? I don't want you to do anything that isn't ethical. I don't want you to get in trouble." Elliot realized he actually liked the idea that Ted was willing to risk everything for him.

"Never mind that. All that's important now is to get you out of here."

"I am telling you the truth, Ted. You must believe me; I had nothing to do with any of this."

"OK. OK. Of course I believe you. In a little while I'll see what the police have got on you. First tell me about the woman."

"I don't know…" Elliot had to think fast to construct an innocent story that would not imply any romantic connection. He knew that soon the evidence would be revealed to Ted and he needed to think quickly, but at this point he decided to say as little as possible. "This Lindsey…a beautiful woman…a few months ago, she came to my clinic with her mother. I removed a cancerous tumor from her mother's stomach. Of all people… I can't believe I got myself into this mess," Elliot said as if getting angry at himself. "Anyway, at first she started coming to my office more frequently, talking about her mother's prognosis, but slowly it developed on a more personal level. To tell you the truth, I found myself growing attracted to her and enjoyed knowing her, but that's all there was." Moving uncomfortably in his seat, he added, as if he just remembered, "Oh yes...I did go to her home a few times to visit her mother."

Ted tried hard not to show his emotions and said nothing. He felt anger mix with satisfaction at seeing Elliot struggle to cover his lies. *You motherfucker*, he thought. *Do not feed me lies. I know you have been seeing her romantically. All this time you have been preaching to me about my promiscuous life style. And now look at your pathetic lies, your pretentious innocent face. If I didn't know better I would be tempted to believe you.*

"But you never do house calls..." Ted said quietly.

"Not as a rule. And after a few months I realized I couldn't afford to get involved in anything that would risk my position, my family and Ruth. I decided to stop seeing her outside of my office."

Ted could not hold back his emotions any longer. He needed to excuse himself to go to the bathroom. *Elliot was going to end the relationship with Lindsey*, he thought bitterly. *If I just waited a little longer she might have ended up with me. Dammit, Elliot didn't even want Lindsey anymore but she was still pursuing him. I was doing everything to win her heart and got flat-out rejected.*

Ted waited in line at the urinal, disgusted by the excessive urine on the floor and the need to share this kind of activity with other people. He washed his face with cold water, agitated by the lack of paper to wipe his hands. He still felt the hurt and the jealously that surfaced again. *Everything falls right into Elliot's lap. He doesn't have to do anything for it.* He breathed slowly to calm down before returning to Elliot. Seeing Elliot sitting behind bars with his head lowered as if the world had fallen on him, Ted could not help feeling sorry for his nemesis. He felt a mixture of love and envy that surfaced with equal force and intensity.

On the way back to Elliot, Ted got hold of himself and reverted to his friendly and professional disposition. He greeted Elliot with a pat on his shoulder. "Hey buddy, cheer up. Like you said, it's some kind of mix-up. We'll get you out of here in no time. Let me talk to the police and I'll straighten out this mess. First of all I'll get you out on bail, and then I'll take you home."

Elliot looked at his old friend with thankful eyes. "Thanks. I don't want to stay in this stinking place a moment longer than necessary."

Ted went to talk to the officer in charge. The police station was humming with activity. He passed criminals with bulging muscles and elaborately decorated tattoos that covered large parts of their bodies. Prostitutes with minimal clothing were being detained for twenty-four hours. Lawyers were dealing with their clients. Ted had to remind the desk officer a few times of his request to see the officer in charge. Finally, he was led to a small office at the end of the corridor.

Ted felt repulsion looking at the heavy-bellied sergeant who sunk his bulk into the cheap leather chair behind the dusty crowded desk. He was talking on the telephone, smoking a cigarette, not bothering to pause a moment to invite him to sit. Ted sat down in the chair, uninvited, and waved his hand in front of the officer's face to make his presence known. When the officer finally hung up the phone, Ted, in an authoritative tone, demanded to know what was going on. The officer looked calmly at Ted with eyes that expressed boredom, and dismissed his arrogant demeanor. He brought Elliot's file up on the computer screen and studied it for a moment.

"We have strong evidence that your client was involved in the murder of Ms. Lindsey Anderson on the twenty-eighth of October in her SoHo apartment, at Prince Street and Broadway," he said, reading the charges.

"I would like to see the arrest warrant."

The officer made a copy and handed it to Ted, saying, "Issued by the criminal court."

"You know very well that upon arrest, you must bring him immediately to the local criminal court," Ted rejoined, trying to intimidate the officer.

"We know…"

"My client has the right to see an arraignment judge right away," Ted interrupted.

"At this moment all I can tell you is that the investigation is continuing but it does not look good for your client. From what I see, evidence has been collected connecting your client to the scene of the crime."

"Well, we'll see about that. I am here to have bail set and to get him out of here."

"Sorry, but no can do," the officer replied, trying to punch back at the arrogant lawyer like a needle poking into a balloon. "First we are going to hold him for the usual twenty-four hours. If I'm not mistaken, the paper work is on its way over so we can hold him as long as we need to."

Ted knew from previous experience that presenting himself with authority usually intimidated the police officers. So he demanded, "I want to talk to the senior officer, someone who is in charge of the case and knows exactly what is going on."

The sergeant had seen this kind of show before and raised his voice. "Tonight, I'm the only one you can talk to in this station. Tomorrow morning you can go to the judge and make any demand or request you'd like." He got up and opened the door. "I have pressing business to attend to. Please excuse me."

Ted left the room, angry with himself for having entered into an unnecessary power match. He did not like cops and in court he tried to tear their image to shreds whenever he could. *You must preserve your energy for the real battle*, he mused.

He returned to Elliot with the bad news and saw the desolation on Elliot's face. "Is there anything we can do?"

"I tried, but until tomorrow morning…"

"This is the first time I've been arrested. To stay here all night is awful. It will devastate my wife. It will kill my father if he hears about any of this."

"Listen buddy, the police report did not say much. They are

still gathering evidence and they aren't revealing it to me. It's the usual twenty-four hour intimidation, just a tactic of their investigation. Remember; do not say anything without me present."

Elliot realized there was nothing else that could be done. "Please call Ruth and ask her not to tell anybody, including the children, and to call the clinic and ask my secretary to cancel all my appointments for tomorrow. Don't tell her any more then she needs to know."

"Tomorrow morning I'll talk to the arraignment judge and straighten out this mess," Ted reassured his friend. The two men hugged briefly. "Don't worry. Twenty-four hours will pass fast."

2

After Ted left, an officer returned to handcuff Elliot and lead him back to his cell. Elliot was relieved that he did not have to share the cell with anyone. He sat on the bunk, bent his head over his hands, and felt the shame and degradation of his situation. He lay down on the hard mattress and stared at the torn mattress above, lost in the events since his arrest.

Elliot thought of Ruth, whom he would soon have to face. When the police came to his home to arrest him, he was glad she had been in a meeting for one of her charities. She did not have to witness the horror of his being arrested, a month after Lindsey's murder. It happened on a Wednesday afternoon, when he was off from work. Elliot had just returned home from rounds at the hospital when two policemen rang the doorbell and presented him with the arrest warrant, charging him with the murder of Lindsey Anderson. They were polite as they read him his rights and handcuffed him, warning him that anything he said might be held against him. He was in shock as they led him to the police car and drove him to the police station.

Elliot felt shame when he noticed a few of his neighbors peeking through their windows and watching with astonished faces as he was driven away. He sat in the backseat feeling numb, watching the streets passing by as if in a dream. It was as if there were two distinct worlds, one outside the car window with all its activities, and another completely separate reality inside the car with him as the invisible observer. Then he became oblivious to the details of the outer world and stayed frozen in a panic that lasted until they arrived at the police station.

Ruth doesn't deserve any of this. She is a wonderful, loyal wife, he thought, trying to understand how he could have fallen into such irresponsible behavior and carried on an affair with Lindsey. *My life was fulfilling and full of accomplishments. I was happy. I have two wonderful children and a successful practice. I love my job and my patients. What else could anyone wish for?*

How could I have fallen under the seductive spell of Lindsey just like a teenage boy? She was the one who pursued me; she gets everything she wants. But I was a willing participant. I shouldn't blame anyone for my stupidity. Only Lindsey could be the woman that could take me away from all that but I made the wrong choice getting involved. What a crazy six months it's been. I was like a drug addict coming back to get a fix and Lindsey could really deliver the merchandise. Now she is dead and instead of everything being over, it's the beginning of hell for me.

The first time I fall into cheating and I get caught, Elliot realized bitterly. *Ted has being doing it for years and never has to pay for any consequences.* Elliot knew that Ruth never liked Ted. She did not approve of his lifestyle, although she tried not to show it. She strongly believed that once you commit to a relationship, you should be loyal and that marriage should be lasting. Would she leave him if she found out about the affair?

He was hoping Ted would get him out of the situation quickly without anyone other than Ruth finding out. *No,* Elliot thought frightfully. *I'm going to deny any involvement with Lindsey. I know Ruth, she'll believe me. She always has. But I never had to lie to her.* He shook off his doubts. *I must make sure that everyone, including Ruth and especially Ted, believes I didn't have an affair with Lindsey.*

Elliot painfully remembered how degraded he felt when he arrived at the police station and had to call Ted, begging him to come quickly. He was fingerprinted like a common criminal. The officer held his hand as if it was a foreign object and pressed it into the inkpads. His mug shot was taken with an identity number in front of his chest just like he'd seen in the movies. His humanity was stripped, layer by layer, as the policemen moved him through the motions, as if on a production line. At the end of the arrest proceedings he was led to the interrogation room for questioning.

The team, headed by a lantern-jawed Detective Benjamin Sills, had apparently been gathering evidence and piecing clues together for the past twenty seven days. Sills coordinated his team between many different disciplines to provide expertise in constructing a theory of probable motive and determining the killer. To aid with the investigation, Sills had called in a special psychological team from the FBI to construct a profile of the murderer. Although there was a trace of drug use in the apartment, they ruled out a drug-related homicide. The report had supported initial suspicions that the murder was caused in a moment of rage by someone who knew the victim and, in fact, was probably her lover. The team had worked hard to gather sufficient evidence to present for Elliot's arrest warrant.

Elliot was not aware that Detective Sills had been on the police force for thirty-five years and had an impressive record of solved cases. Detective Sills felt the pressure from the brass and was determined to bring this case to successful a completion. So far it seemed that things were unfolding to his satisfaction, as they had since the night he arrived at Lindsey's apartment as chief detective. Margaret Anderson, the victim's mother and the one who found her, was crying softly. She told him what she had witnessed when she entered the apartment. After he spoke to the first officer on the scene, he climbed upstairs to the living area, taking in the unusual place and carefully observing anything that could give him a clue as to what had happened.

He remembered his first impression of the crime scene, looking at the beautiful woman lying lifeless on the couch. At first glance it did not appear as if a crime had been committed, but then he saw the broken chair and the unnatural manner in which Lindsey was lying. His gut feeling convinced him that there was more there than met the eye. Following the letter of the law, he knew that only the coroner was allowed to touch the body. He called the coroner's office, eager to get the autopsy results. He gave the order to secure the site properly and made sure the photographer didn't touch anything as he took the necessary photographs. As more investigators and crime personnel arrived, he made sure all crime scene procedures were strictly followed, so as to avoid any contamination of the evidence.

When Detective Sills first looked at Elliot through the one-way window of the interrogation room, he tried to form a strong first impression. The small interrogation room had no windows and bright lighting. It was sparsely furnished with only a wooden table and a few chairs, creating an atmosphere of intimidation. Sills observed Elliot sitting alone for a long time, looking for clues in his body language and demeanor, trying to decide on the best first approach. Elliot was handsome and still looked impressive, even in this compromising situation. The few strands of gray hair added to his respectable look. His blue eyes were kind and sad. His long fingers seemed like those of a pianist.

Elliot did not know he was being watched. Sills noticed how Elliot sat with his arms and legs crossed as if trying to take up less physical space, of how he was trying to control his nervousness. He looked at the door too often, breathing deeply, preparing to face his interrogator. *He is not behaving like an innocent man*, Sills thought. *He is definitely not an average street criminal. He is a doctor used to being in command.* Benjamin looked at Elliot's top-quality navy pinstriped suit and very expensive watch. *This is a wealthy man and I need to be careful; he is going to be all over me with his lawyers. It's going to be a high profile case.*

Detective Sills wondered if he had the right man. *Could this man have killed in cold blood? Can what seems on the surface to be a rational man, underneath be someone who killed a woman? What caused such a rage?* He reminded himself that too often looks were deceiving. Benjamin entered the room and shook Elliot's hand.

"My name is Detective Benjamin Sills and I'm in charge of this investigation."

Elliot was surprised when Detective Sills entered the room. He had a different image in mind of what his interrogator would look like. He had imagined someone more threatening. Sills was strong-featured but resembled an all-American grandfather. His high forehead and warm blue eyes were accompanied by a pleasant smile. Elliot stood up to return Sill's handshake, then folded his arms tight on his chest as he sat down.

"Cigarette?" Sills said with a friendly smile.

"No thanks, I don't smoke."

"Do you mind?" Not waiting for a response, Sills lit his cigarette, knowing full well that the doctor could have protested, but he didn't dare. This was another clue for Sills to use to determine Elliot's level of confidence and possible guilt. "If it's all right with you I'd like to ask a few questions."

"I was advised by my lawyer not to say anything without him being present."

A smartass who learns fast to hide beyond his lawyer's back, Sills surmised. *It's not going to be that easy. I need an effective approach.* He pouted and knotted his brow. "Is that because you have something to hide? Do we really need your lawyer present for only a few questions? I'm only interested in getting your side of the story."

"No, but…" Elliot said, his eyes darting from side to side. "I don't need to deny or to admit anything without my lawyer present."

To deny or to admit, huh? A sentence like that shows me this guy has something to hide, or he would protest being wrongfully accused. His avoidance of eye contact is a sign of deception, Sills noted. "Look Dr. Barrett, we can hold you here for questioning for as long as we like. I'm sure that would not be to your advantage." Sills immediately realized he had touched a sensitive nerve. Elliot's face reddened and his posture became more defensive.

Ah, his weak point is his reputation. Sills decided to take advantage of the moment, leaned closer toward Elliott and with a persuasive voice tried to reason with him. "We have enough evidence to tie you to the murder. As a matter of fact, the paperwork is being processed at this very moment. Believe me, it doesn't give me any pleasure to hold you here," Benjamin took a long pause, staring directly at Elliot. He knew that his proximity added to Elliot's level of discomfort, creating a kind of mental claustrophobia.

The silence was thick and long. "Is there anything you want to get off your chest?" Sills saw how the question threw Elliot for a loop. Regardless of Elliot's 'No' answer, he could read the defensive clue of Elliot's body turning sideways, as if trying to dodge the facts.

"You read me my rights. I don't have to say anything. My lawyer is on his way over here and then I'll take his advice."

"Is that what you were told?" Sills created a doubtful grin on his face, as if pretending the information was wrong, knowing full well that Elliot was within his legal rights. "That's your right, Dr. Barrett. You are under no legal obligation to answer, but..." Sills saw that his pressure was not yielding results, but he had gotten what he wanted from his initial round of questioning. Elliot's behavior pointed to his guilt. He called the guard to take Elliot to his cell.

Not knowing the time in the windowless cell, Elliot estimated it was past midnight.

He lay exhausted, his mind continuing to race relentlessly. Time passed slowly. He tossed in bed but could not find a comfortable position. The mildewed mattress was thin and rough and metal slats poked at his body. The commode was overflowing even before he came into the cell, and released a sharp, choking odor that filled the cell. He couldn't relieve himself in these foul and filthy conditions.

Before dawn his body was aching and he began to tremble. The physical and emotional pain was intolerable. In spite of his repulsion, he forced himself to use the toilet and felt he had reached the lowest point in his life. He huddled in a fetal position and tried to get into a mental numbness to escape the pain, but to no avail. Elliot could not hold back his emotions any longer and started crying. He did not let the sound become audible for fear he would be heard. He covered his face with his hands and felt the tears rolling down, out of control. The truth of the situation hit him with all its power and there was no way to escape to find any comfort.

At six o'clock in the morning, he received a tray of unappetizing food, which he ignored. Then, two policemen opened his cell and led him back to the interrogation room. Benjamin was already waiting for him, smoking his cigarette, adding to the suffocation of the already stifling room. Benjamin knew Elliot was at his lowest point and wanted to take advantage of the situation. The mental pressure and unpleasant physical conditions which he felt must be applied were unfortunate parts of his job, but he knew that sometimes they were effective ways to provoke confessions.

Detective Sills was going to use one of his soft and effective techniques. He wanted to create a rapport and trust, to build a psychological bridge. The first round of questions he asked restricted Elliot to truthful answers, questions that were not related to the case and were of a friendly, personal exchange. He asked about the nature of his occupation and even complimented Elliot's role in society. Sills knew that the best approach with Elliot would not involve force.

To reduce Eliot's apprehension, Sills turned the attention to himself and told Elliot he was close to his retirement and really didn't like to put people like Elliot in such a situation. He promised he would try to help him as much as he could. "Last night I requested special treatment for you. I asked the warden to put you in a cell by yourself. Of course, I wouldn't like you to be treated like a common street criminal," he paused, matching Elliot's gestures, posture and tone of voice, with the intention of creating a subliminal connection between them.

"Thanks, I do appreciate it," Elliot said as a flash of the dreadful night ran through his mind.

"I've had a few cases similar to yours, and I know that anyone under duress can make a mistake." He opened his palms and raised his shoulders as if he empathized with Elliot. "Maybe it was an accident. I can understand you didn't plan on this happening. Things just got out of control, right? You didn't do it intentionally, right?"

"I thought my lawyer should be present during all questioning," Elliot felt the pressure build through his body as he sat frozen in his position.

"Look, any question you don't feel comfortable with you don't have to answer." Benjamin continued his soft approach and remembered Elliot's soft spot from yesterday's interrogation. "You are a doctor. I'm sure you do not want your life to be disrupted any more than necessary. I know you want to get on with your life when all this is over. You know it could be altered for the worse with ripples that could affect your work and your family for a long time." Sills saw the immediate effect on Elliot's increasingly fearful face.

"I need to consult with my lawyer before I can answer any questions," Elliot sounded almost apologetic. Benjamin felt he was getting effective. It was the point in the interrogation when he needed to give Elliot a stronger incentive to speak. He knew he was breaking the rule by not responding to Elliot's plea for legal representation, but he needed to establish a concrete personal verification of Elliot's involvement in the murder. It would make his investigation and it was necessary for the prosecutor in the courtroom.

"Look, I'm sure you would like to wash up, shave, take a good shower, eat a good meal, sleep in a decent bed," Benjamin knew that involving all the senses, the visual, auditory and kinesthetic, would make that experience as real as possible. That would make Elliot think emotionally instead of logically. "All I need is…"

The door suddenly opened and a uniformed cop looked inside but immediately realized he made a mistake and retreated quickly. *I will kill that man*, Sills thought. Looking with disappointment at Elliot, he realized he had missed a golden opportunity.

Elliot, as if entering back to the real world, remembered Ted's instructions not to say anything. He had just escaped a well-positioned snare. "All I can say is that without my lawyer present I will not say a word," he said, crossing his arms and legs tight to his body.

3

Ted called Elliot's house from his car and recognized Ruth's energetic voice, still tinged with a Texas accent.

"Ruth, this is Ted..."

"Elliot isn't home yet, he's running late from his..."

"Yes I know. I need to talk to you personally. I'm not far from your house."

"What's the matter? Where is Elliot?" Ruth wondered at the strange request.

Ted had never come to the house without Elliot being there.

"I can't talk on the phone."

"Is everything all right with Elliot?"

"He's fine; I'll be there in ten minutes."

Ted drove onto Park Avenue then turned left on 62nd Street, for the few blocks to Elliot's warmly-lit brownstone. What a place for the elite, where the greed of New York high society resides! *The whole area smells of money and the rich use their tax write-offs to keep some of the public institutions alive. My place on the West Side is too parvenu for them. Let them define themselves by their addresses. Can't beat my apartment's great view of Central Park.*

When Ted arrived, Ruth greeted him at the door looking worried. "Something bad has happened."

"Elliot is fine. He asked me to come over and explain to you personally, so you won't be worried," Ted calmly told her. "There is some kind of mix-up. He got involved..."

"What are you saying? What kind of mix-up?" Ruth was frantic.

"Let's sit down," Ted said, leading Ruth to the well-furnished living room. She wore a dress too conservative to his liking, as if she just came out of church. She was tall with a gentle, pretty face and a pert nose. Green eyes and blonde hair, collected neatly at the back of her head, lent her an aristocratic look. She was always active and moved swiftly, which made her look younger than her forty-five years.

"Tell me where Elliot is," she said impatiently.

"Elliot is in the police station for questioning. He will have to stay there for the night but tomorrow morning I'm going to get him released."

"Questioning... In jail...?" Ruth sank into the couch, her face pale. "What do the police want with him?"

Ted felt the slight pleasure of Ruth's humiliation. He knew that Ruth tried hard not to show her dislike of him. He was Elliot's best friend but she felt as if he stood in her way. Ruth did not want to share Elliot with anyone.

"They said he was mixed up in a murder..." Ted realized the danger of elaborating but could not retreat.

"Murder? A murder? Ted, what in heaven's name are you talking about?" Ruth screamed with shock. "There must be a mistake. You mean malpractice with a patient?"

"No." Ted paused trying to choose the right words. He noticed Ruth's widened eyes as she anticipated his explanation. "Elliot was... well, the police said Elliot was involved with another woman..."

"With another woman? Is that a joke? That is just impossible." Ruth's high pitched voice got an octave higher. "Elliot would never..." her face was blushed with anger. "That just could not be."

Ted felt some perverse satisfaction and decided to ease the situation. "That is just what the police claim. It's probably some kind of a mix-up. Don't worry, tomorrow I'll know the details and get him back home. And by the way Elliot has asked not to notify anyone yet. And please make the proper arrangements with his office for tomorrow."

Ruth tried to question Ted but quickly realized that he did not know many answers. She felt somewhat relieved at Ted's confidence that the matter would be resolved by morning.

Ted left Ruth sitting on the couch in deep thought and saw himself out. *Can I be one of those wives last to know that her husband is having an affair?* Just the thought of it sent sharp pains to her chest. She tried to reexamine the past to see if there was any hint in Elliot's behavior, but found none. During their twenty-one years of marriage, Ruth and Elliot had no real cause for friction. Occasionally there was an argument that had to do with how the children should be raised. There were a few disagreements that surfaced about how the clinic should be managed. But they had come to agreements on dividing responsibilities between them. There could be a discussion about any subject, but the final decision would be in the hands of the person in charge of that particular task.

After learning the horrifying news about Elliot, Ruth sat for hours on the couch. Still tearful, she washed up and crawled into the large empty bed, touching the space where Elliot usually slept. Stories from wives of other doctors whose life were devastated by their husbands' affairs surfaced in her mind. She could not help thinking about the sad marriages of some of her friends that ended in divorce and the destruction of families—wives who worked hard to support their husbands through the difficult years of medical school, helped them establish successful private practices and kept up with the house and a family—wives who arrived in mid-life bitter, lonely and abandoned, because they had given the best time of their lives to the wrong man. To make matters worse, some of the doctors had gone on to marry much younger women, who benefited from the financial gain that was mutually accomplished with their first wife.

Ruth always believed this would never happen to her. She remembered Elliot's explanation that many doctors felt that their youth had been consumed getting through medical school. They wanted to recapture what they had lost. He said some of the doctors sought a divorce because they were used to the power and respect they received in the workplace and had a hard time coming home to the realities of married life.

But Elliot is not that kind of man, Ruth desperately reasoned. *He is shy and never responds flirtatiously to women approaching him. There must be a mistake. There must be a mix-up that will be resolved by tomorrow. It might all be nothing just like Ted said*, Ruth concluded with hope. She thought of Elliot being in his cell and was concerned for his well-being. *I hope he is being treated well*, she thought. *He is too gentle for such an experience.* Her worry turned into feelings of compassion for what Elliot was going through.

Ruth was a dedicated wife and mother. She enjoyed the satisfaction of her children's accomplishments. Jonathan was a sensitive young man with many talents and good grades in college. Now in his third year at Duke, he had changed majors a few times, trying to find the right professional track. He would not yield to Elliot's pressure to go to medical school and join the practice, saying he would take all the time necessary to find what he wanted. Caroline, on the other hand, showed a strong determination and knew exactly what she was going to do. She was planning to finish her undergraduate degree at Brown and go on to medical school. Since Caroline left home for her first year at college six months ago, Ruth had become busier at work and to fill the void, began remodeling the house. She had felt the same emptiness when their son Jonathan left for college three years earlier, but this time it was more severe. The house felt quiet and the daily chores diminished now that it was just Elliot and her, living without their kids. Ruth had too much free time on her hands and decided to take on more responsibility at work and to join a few charity organizations.

Elliot was busy at work and a few nights a week brought paperwork home with him. During the week they spent quiet evenings at home, enjoying Ruth's home-cooked meals, watching television and relaxing in each other's company. On weekends they would attend the Metropolitan Opera or see a show Off-Broadway, visit friends or drive to Boston to visit Elliot's family. A few times a year they flew to visit the children and went to visit Ruth's family in Texas for family events. When the children were back from college, they would all take a vacation at a beautiful resort and spend quality time together. It was a great and fulfilling life.

They had been happily married for twenty-one years. Ruth left Fort Worth to attend Cornell to complete her master's degree in hospital administration after earning her undergraduate degree at the University of Texas. She had loved Austin, and planned to return to make Austin her home. The city had a warm sense of place and offered a variety of activities. It was small enough to feel intimate but large enough to offer the excitement of a diverse and stimulating population. The green hills and large lakes west of the city offered outdoor activity close by.

Ruth came from an affluent family, raised on the golden rule and the principles of the Baptist church they attended regularly. Her father had a strong work ethic, was a rancher and taught Sunday school. Her mother was busy raising her children, Ruth being the oldest of four girls. They lived on a large cattle ranch and learned the value of a hard day's work.

Her first year in New York was difficult. The contrast between this metropolis and her hometown and college town felt like moving to a foreign country. Ruth was busy with school demands and trying to adjust to the fast pace and rudeness of New York, so different from her native, laid-back Texas. She missed the vast spaces and the open blue sky, the mild winters, in contrast to the freezing cold of New York. She missed the hours of riding with her beloved quarter horse Betsy, and mostly she longed for the intimate time she shared with her three sisters and family.

When she met Elliot, a brilliant, shy guy who was gentle and confident, she fell in love immediately. During their first year together Elliot was buried in his medical training. On the few weekends they would drive to the countryside up north where she could temporarily fulfill her yearning for the open spaces, naked sky, and love of nature.

When Ruth graduated she accepted a job at Mount Sinai Hospital while Elliot finished his residency. Once Elliot finished his training, they were married back in Boston. The wedding was a spectacular display of wealth and lavishness. Ruth looked stunning in a wedding gown created by a well-known designer. It took six children to carry the twelve-foot train. Elliot looked charming in his specially-made tuxedo. Ruth's sisters stood at her side as bridesmaids with Debbie, the sister to whom she was closest, as matron of honor. Ted was at Elliot's side as best man.

Senators and dignitaries from Boston and Texas were part of the large guest list. It was an event for Elliot's family to show off their fortune and the pretty new addition to the family. Ruth's wealthy but unassuming family was proud of Elliot's accomplishments and rejoiced at the thought of his future career.

They moved to a grand brownstone on the East Side, known as The Treadwell Farm Historic District, once home to Eleanor Roosevelt and Montgomery Clift. The brownstone, still their home, was on a tree-lined street and had four stories and a basement. They loved the location on East 62nd St., between Second and Third Avenues, a few blocks from Elliot's clinic. His parents purchased the brownstone as part of a wedding gift that also included a large sum of money from the family trust.

Two years later Ruth had Jonathan. She stopped working and devoted herself to caring for her family. One year later she had Caroline. She respected Elliot's agnostic view of religion, and he did not object when she took the children to church on holidays. He enjoyed the atmosphere and festivities she created around the house on the holidays and encouraged the children to choose their religious affiliation. They were a modern family.

When Caroline was five years old and began school, Ruth began helping Elliot establish his private practice. With Ruth's skills as an administrator, Elliot's connections and his success as a cancer surgeon, his practice grew quickly.

Ted became a part of Ruth's life owing to his friendship with

Elliot. She soon discovered that Ted's lifestyle and views contradicted hers, to say the least. His promiscuity and relationships with other women appalled her, even before Ted was married. He was too aggressive and ambitious and would risk anything to win. Ruth came from many past generations of wealth and enjoyed the quality that money provided without the need for pretensions. Ted's relentless attempts to express his material gains as the measure of success and accomplishments went against everything she had been raised to believe. She recognized his talent as a lawyer but did not respect his unrelenting ambition.

Ruth had hoped that after they married, Elliot's connection with Ted would fade away. She tried to tell Elliott how she felt, but he shrugged it off, saying that how Ted ran his life was his own business. Ruth told Elliott that she was not interested in participating in their relationship, and he respected her request. A few times a week Elliott met Ted to play racquetball or for drinks.

Years later, at the age of thirty-five, Ted married Heather, a flight attendant he met on one of his business trips. Heather was good hearted and Ruth liked her. Occasionally the four of them went out together. They visited each other's homes infrequently and shared short holiday vacations.

As the hours went by and the morning sun rose, Ruth remembered these details of her life and tossed in bed restlessly, unable to sleep, wondering how the next day would unfold.

4

Before going to bed, Ted prepared his notes for the confrontation with the District attorney in front of the arraignment judge. He got up in the morning full of energy and ready for the day. Heather was still sleeping. He washed and shaved and entered his closet to choose his clothes for the day, a ritual he enjoyed.

Scanning the full row of shirts, he chose a strong blue Armani button-down that went well with a gray double-breasted suit. Having selected a red print silk tie, he looked at himself in the floor-length mirror, and was pleased.

On the stairway leading to the courthouse, he met George Goodman and learned that he would be representing the DA's office in Elliot's case. In the past they had tried a few court cases together. Ted had lost only one. He respected George's argumentative skills and knowledge of the law. George had graduated from Yale Law and Ted thought he showed promise of becoming a great lawyer and fulfilling his ambition to become a State Supreme Court judge.

He was thirty-four years old but appeared older, with a receding hairline and a large belly. He often didn't match his clothes colors and wore ill-fitting suits that made him seem shorter than his height of five-foot eight inches. His rushed shaving was evident in the few whiskers on his cheeks. But Ted loved his smiling, warm, brown eyes that showed his goodness and wit and truly expressed George's personality.

Ted tapped George's shoulder in a friendly gesture and George responded with an arm over Ted's shoulder. "What's up, George? Come to be nailed by me again?"

"Don't bet on it, Ted. This time I have some ammunition."

"Stop your bullshit, George. Smart-aleck Jew, you've got nothing."

George made a face as if he was insulted by Ted's remark but then smiled quickly. "We will see. We will see."

"Hey, did you hear what happened with the Whitman case last week?" Ted teased.

"Not bad for a Polack, not bad. You won again," George responded with a smile that said 'I got you back'. "I wouldn't have let you off the hook that easy,"

"Let's go inside. It's getting cold for this time of the year," Ted suggested.

"Yes, it's El Nino this year, this is only the beginning. It's supposed to be crazy weather pattern all over the world. About twelve years ago storms did a helluva lot of damage. I'm serious Ted. We are all responsible for this shit. We are destroying the rain forest, and with all this pollution and ozone depletion we're responsible for the earth."

"Lighten up, George. You're always worried about this kind of thing."

"Unless people are affected personally, nobody gives a damn. When they wake up it might be too late. And you know what? America is using more energy per capita than any country in the world." They arrived together in front of the tall heavy courtroom doors.

"After you," Ted said, and pointed to the courtroom door.

Ted loved the atmosphere in the courtroom with its large rooms and high ceilings, the stained wooden doors and molding, the thick marble floor and large windows. It lent a sense of place, power and respectability. Ted cherished the courthouse where all his faculties were challenged. His attention was on full alert, and his skills and senses were razor sharp.

Ted and George sat at their opposing desks. The American Judicial Method—justice by adversity—had begun. The two sides would present their best arguments and the jury would announce the final verdict. George started by explaining to the arraignment judge the implication of his case. He argued for the state to expand Elliot's jail time for seven more days to allow the police to continue their investigation. He argued that they were dealing with a murder and the police already had plenty of evidence to keep him behind bars.

Ted argued that the state had not shown any concrete evidence, only circumstantial evidence. He said that Elliot had never been arrested before. He stated that the damage to Elliot's name and reputation as a respected doctor in the community would be tarnished beyond repair and that the state did not need to worry about Elliot not showing up for further proceedings.

The hearing was short. After a few questions, the judge asked for arguments from Ted and George. He ruled that bail was set in the amount of $250,000 which would deter Elliot from not showing up. The judge had spoken the final word.

After the judge left the room, Ted turned to George with a pointed finger, "One to zero in my favor."

"It's just the beginning," George smiled. He pointed his finger back at Ted, emulating a pistol. "Boom," he said, laughing. Ted pointed his finger at George and then at his temple "Boom, boom is what you are going to need to do to yourself at the end." Both were laughing as they left the courtroom.

With a satisfied smile, Ted drove to the police station to release Elliot. *I need Elliot back at home and working again so he will believe he is completely free. I am going to pacify him by assuring him that everything is all right, and then I can manipulate the course of events my way.* With even more conviction he thought, *I can't afford to have any attention pointed in my direction.*

At the police station he greeted Elliot with a hug. Elliott looked tired and ill-kempt, with a one-day growth of beard, but seemed encouraged. "Thanks Ted. I wouldn't have survived another night in that place. Take me home, I need a shower badly."

"What did I say to you yesterday, huh? Piece of cake. You're out, aren't you?" Ted said. "Go home, shower and then get back to work. I'll handle everything from now on."

"The detective tried hard to force a confession from me."

"Did you…?"

"No, no, but to tell you the truth this detective was clever."

"They've got all kind of tricks up their sleeves, don't they?"

"Detective Sills really does."

Elliot got into Ted's red Jaguar. It still smelled new. He enjoyed the last few days of Fall before the long cold of the New York winter began. All his senses were heightened. He felt the warm sunshine on his face and everything seemed more alive. The Jag passed through the dark shadows cast by the skyscrapers before turning on to the FDR highway going uptown. The shimmering rays on the East River mesmerized him. They passed the South Street Seaport complex full of shops, museums, and markets packed with tourists. They drove under the Brooklyn Bridge, showing old glory and might, with the Gothic towers anchor each end as a gateway to the island.

Out of Eliot's silent mind, a flash of realization sparked. It was the first time he realized and appreciated what freedom meant. He had taken life for granted. Everything had always come easily to him. He never had to stop and think about being free. Or was he?

Elliot glanced at Ted and realized that Ted had real freedom. Ted did what he wanted without accounting to anybody. Ted could make any move he liked without needing approval from his father. Sure, there were benefits Elliot enjoyed, such as great material gain and stature in the community. His father paid his way, bought him a house, and placed him on a social level that opened doors. Ted, on the other hand, was a self-made man and accomplished everything on his own. He bought his freedom by his own actions.

Elliot always had to make concessions to his parents. Medical school was not his first choice. He wanted to be an archeologist, but his father objected, saying he was expecting more of his son and had planned for him to be a doctor. Elliot did not express any objections, although he desperately wanted to. On a few occasions he felt he was trapped in a tight vise but could not or did not have the ability to get out. He wanted to please his father.

Now more than ever, Elliot appreciated his long friendship with Ted. At the worst time of his life Ted had come to his rescue. He literally bailed him out and was there on his side with help and encouragement.

Elliot's thoughts carried him back thirty years ago to his undergraduate days at Columbia. He met Ted as a freshman, and they lived in the student dorm next door to each other. They had remained best friends. The second year they rented an apartment on 102nd Street along the bank of the Hudson. Ted's strong ambition to become a well-known criminal lawyer had impressed Elliot. Ted received a tuition scholarship but he had to take a student loan and worked to pay the rest of his expenses. On weekends and vacations he was a waiter in a fancy restaurant on Fifth Avenue.

Ted completed his undergraduate degree in three years instead of four, at the top of his class. Columbia Law School, his first choice, accepted him. After graduation, he was immediately recruited as a defense criminal lawyer by a large Manhattan firm. His success in the courtroom soon earned him a partnership. In a short time he bought a nice apartment on West 68th Street, overlooking Central Park. In later years he purchased the adjacent apartment, and with major remodeling combined it into one space. Ted found great excitement and interest in his work and, with the same zeal, plunged into the nightlife of Manhattan.

Elliot loved Ted's passion for life and the energy he displayed. Elliot was shy. In some ways he disapproved of Ted's treatment of women, but always enjoyed his erotic stories and the bizarre experiences he shared. The sexual revolution was already under way and Ted embraced it with open arms. Elliot's connections helped him dodge the draft and Ted was never called to serve. Both were glad to be saved from serving in the dreadful war in Vietnam.

Now Ted glanced at Elliot and was puzzled by his expression.

What is he thinking? Is he thinking of Lindsey? Is he afraid to face Ruth? Maybe he is thinking of what he will tell her. It's going to be difficult to explain the physical evidence found in Lindsey's house.

"Ted, what's going to happen now?" Elliott asked as he woke from his reverie.

"I'm on the top of the situation. They'll continue digging for more evidence. Right now they've got nothing. Worst case scenario, if they feel they got something on you, they will try to take it in front of a grand jury, but I will not let them drag us into court. It will be dismissed and everything will be over."

"Why you are so sure?" Elliot asked, hoping Ted would be right.

"I have dozens of cases I get dismissed before we have to go to court. When they know they don't have enough evidence, they don't want to take the risk of losing. Many things are involved but basically they like to cover their asses."

Ted parked his car in front of Elliot's brownstone. Elliot seemed tense. Ruth ran out the door, rushed to the car and hugged Elliot. She lowered her head through the car window. "Ted, come in and have some coffee." Elliot turned back and repeated. "Yes, that's a good idea. Join us."

"Not right now. I must return to my office. I've lots of things to catch up on. I'll call you later." Ted drove away as Ruth and Elliot waved enthusiastically.

Suddenly Ruth is overly friendly, he thought with irony. *Yesterday, her righteous indignation cracked a bit. We will see how the Texas cowgirl holds up.*

5

Ruth helped Elliot remove his clothing, appalled by the repulsive smell still emanating from his shirt and pants. She drew a hot bath and brought him a towel. Then she watched Elliot concentrate on scrubbing his body thoroughly, as if preparing to enter the operating room. From the first moment she saw him get out of Ted's car, she could sense his extreme preoccupation, and now felt engulfed in an aura of his sadness. Ruth wanted to ask so many questions but knew she must wait.

Elliot scrubbed his body as if he could rid himself of recent memories. He knew Ruth was watching him attentively but pretended not to notice. He couldn't establish eye contact, fearing that she would penetrate right through him and read his thoughts. He was rehearsing possible answers to the hard questions he knew she would ask.

Ruth watched him step out of the bath and noticed how, at forty-eight years old, his six-foot-tall body was in such good shape. His torso was still accented by a well-defined chest, and his long muscular legs gave him the athletic look of a runner. The only slight differences bestowed by the years were gentle wrinkles on the sides of his eyes and the few gray hairs on his temples. His full, shiny dark brown hair was layered in a short cut that complemented his handsome face. Ruth helped wipe his body dry.

"I'll get you some coffee," she said. When she returned Elliot was collapsed on their bed, deep in sleep. *I wanted to talk with him,* she thought with disappointment as she placed the blanket tenderly over Elliot's body. *Many things are not yet clear but they can wait.*

Elliot slept into late evening. Ruth came in a few times and noticed that his sleep was not peaceful. The blanket was pushed aside from the tossing and turning of his body and he slept in a diagonal position. When he finally woke up they sat down to eat dinner. The silence between them was uncomfortable.

"I'm glad you slept so well," Ruth finally said.

"You can't imagine how much I appreciate just sitting here together," Elliot said. He was grateful that she broke the silence.

Ruth felt reluctant to begin her inquiry but the nagging doubts were too powerful. "Elliot, I want to understand … Why did you get arrested?"

"It's all just a big mix-up that'll soon be cleared up."

"I mean, Ted said there was a woman involved…" She didn't want Elliot to think she didn't trust him but Ruth persisted. "But who… that woman who was killed?"

"Her name was Lindsey," said Elliot, ready with a rehearsed explanation. "She's the daughter of a patient of mine. Seven months ago she came to my office with her mother. I removed a malignant tumor from her mother's stomach."

"What does that have to do with the allegations?"

"Well, the police checked her telephone records and found my number there. Ted said the police had constructed a probable profile of the murderer and the police said I fit that profile."

"What are you saying?" Ruth insisted.

"They concluded that I was involved in a crime of passion."

"Crime of passion? Did you have anything…"

"No, no, Ruth. You must believe me. The police have jumped too quickly to the wrong conclusion."

"Look Elliot, it all sounds bizarre. Why you? Why would they get you mixed up in all this?"

"Ted said in a few days it will all be cleared up. It's just a confusion of mistaken identity."

"Why don't the police think it's maybe a robber?"

"Her place was not robbed. She was not raped, and there was

no forced entry. She was suffocated. The police concluded that she knew the person."

Ruth was silent for a moment. "Do they have any witnesses? Someone must have heard or seen something."

"I don't know," Elliot said desperately. "The police are still investigating. The coroner needs to determine the exact cause of death, the exact time. I'm certain they will learn the truth and I'll be cleared," he said with all the persuasive power he could muster, reminding himself to be convincing, even to himself.

"Okay, Elliot. Of course I believe you had nothing to do with the murder. I know for certain you aren't capable of that. You're a doctor, for god sakes. But did you have anything to do with that woman? I must know the truth."

"Ruth, it is very important that you believe me. I only knew her because of her mother. That's all there was," Elliot said firmly.

Ruth came to Elliot and hugged him. She felt his drained body cling to her. "I'm sorry, but I needed that assurance from you," she said. "It's been very hard for me too. I'm sorry I had any doubt."

Elliot held Ruth tightly, not looking at her face to avoid eye contact so she could not see his nakedness. He feared she would be able to see right through him and his deceit could be revealed. They remained fastened in each other's embrace, as if renewing their commitment. Disengaging himself from the hug, he stood in front of the back window, looking outside, feeling numb. He wanted badly to be lost in the empty darkness outside.

Ruth, content with Elliot's response, felt a bit more at ease. She believed that the man she had been living with for the last twenty-one years would not be a coward and would face her truthfully. Elliot had never lied to her or betrayed her.

Elliot felt awful, knowing he was taking advantage of Ruth's innocent heart.

"Are you going to go to work tomorrow?" Ruth asked.

"Yes, of course. Everything will get back to normal."

"Let's go to bed early," Ruth suggested, feeling exhaustion

catch up with her.

"In a while, Ruth, I just woke up. I'll be there a little later."

"Good night, then. Don't come to bed too late."

"I won't. Good night." She went over to him and they kissed good night.

Elliot felt relieved to be left alone. He was not in the habit of lying, especially to Ruth and also to Ted. He felt twisted now in a sequence of events that were spinning out of control like a savage tornado on a route that would have to run its course. Elliot had always considered himself a man of honor, but now he must lie and convince everyone he is telling the truth. He did not like it.

After Ruth went to sleep he fell back into a reverie. He thought of the day, seven months ago, when Lindsey and her mother Margaret Anderson, a sixty-year-old woman, first came to his clinic. Lindsey explained that her mother lived in New Jersey and needed surgery. Margaret would move to Lindsey's apartment in Manhattan so she could care for her. Elliot was highly recommended by one of Lindsey's clients and she hoped he could help her mother. Elliot checked the medical record from her mother's previous doctor and saw an x-ray showing a malignant cancer growth in Margaret's stomach. He said he needed to take few more tests to determine the best course of action.

Lindsey always accompanied her mother on her post-operative visits. At first Elliot had not paid special attention to Lindsey, but she asked him casual questions that caught him off-guard. Elliot began to anticipate their encounters with eager curiosity. Lindsey was a fascinating person with whom he enjoyed these encounters.

During the next few weeks he found himself attracted by her multicolored personality and charm. Lindsey was a striking thirty-six-year-old woman. At five feet eight inches tall, she had a slim body and an erect posture that showed presence and confidence. She was always dressed well but provocatively, with accessories that called attention to her exposed skin and cleavage. Her long, free-flowing brunette hair and accentuated make-up framed a seductive face. Her gray-green eyes were penetrating and focused on him. It was as if he was the only thing that existed. Her voice had a subtle seductive tone and she laughed freely.

Elliot started noticing her advances toward him and was flattered. At first he casually mentioned that he was happily married. Lindsey ignored this information and continued showing interest in him. At one point she suggested they get together for a quiet lunch outside of the hospital. His fascination with her was growing, but he believed he could retreat at any time he chose.

Elliot dismissed his sexual attraction to Lindsey as a natural urge. She offered excitement and company, breaking the routine of his clinic life. He enjoyed the pleasurable tension. He could identify with Ted's stories of the excitement that comes with conquering a new woman.

Elliot learned that Lindsey had an avid interest in art that had started at a young age. Upon graduation from college, she worked for various museums. With her outgoing personality, she formed relationships with a few wealthy people who needed advice on acquiring art for the purpose of investment. Her circle of clients grew and she was hired to go to auctions to purchase art and earned large commissions. After a broad tour of the Far East, she capitalized on her long-standing interest in the art and antiques of Japan and India and the wood carvings of Bali.

One of her clients had connections to City Hall and had given her a tip on Mayor Koch's initiative for TriBeCa and SoHo. He said it would formulate a real estate aphorism. The city planning department soon rezoned the SoHo business district to become a place for artists to live, work, display and sell their art. Lindsey bought a cast-iron facade building and converted the first floor into a unique art gallery. The second floor was converted to a living area that was connected to the third floor bedroom loft.

Elliot accepted Lindsey's invitation to visit her art gallery. She wanted to show him art and antiques from the Far East that she had described so passionately. Elliot had agreed.

Elliot looked at the clock and saw that it was after midnight. He needed to sleep, but he was not tired. Ruth woke up and noticed Elliot was not in bed. She came to the living room and saw him sitting where she had left him. "What are you doing? You must go to sleep, it's really late," she said, half asleep. Elliot got up and followed her to the bedroom.

6

Elliot woke up feeling drained and exhausted. For most of the night he had dozed on and off. When he finally managed to fall asleep, the nagging sound of the alarm clock soon woke him. He forced himself out of bed and took a shower, hoping to shed the heaviness he felt. He stalled so he would not have to speak with Ruth, who was already in the kitchen preparing breakfast. This morning he decided to drive to work instead of taking his usual walk. He entered the kitchen, grabbed a croissant and kissed Ruth on the cheek. "I'm already late," Elliot said in a hurry, and left before Ruth could object to his departure.

After arriving at the hospital he started his morning rounds. Passing from one patient to the other, Elliot could block out interfering thoughts by giving full attention to his work. Generally, he noted what staff members and patients told him about their lives and families. As he proceeded, he would ask about details he remembered from his notes. Patients and staff members were always amazed and flattered that Elliot remembered and paid such personal attention to them.

When he arrived at his office, his secretary Mary told him that the police had been there the day before and asked questions regarding Mrs. Anderson and her daughter.

"They wanted to know if I knew anything that could help them in regard to Lindsey's death. I told them that besides my professional encounter with Mrs. Anderson and her daughter, I didn't know a thing."

"They asked me too," Elliot said trying to sound extemporaneous. "I spent a few hours in the police station yesterday. That's why we needed to cancel my appointments.

The police are investigating all leads."

"How tragic, she was such a beautiful woman," Mary said.

"Yes, very tragic," Elliot said escaping Mary's scrutinizing eyes by walking to his office.

Of course Elliot did not have anything to do with the killing, Mary reasoned. *But they definitely had something going on between them.* She had noticed the frequent calls from Lindsey, which he received only in his office. The few times she entered the office to give him some files, he stopped talking on the phone and she felt his uneasiness. Having worked for Elliot for eleven years, she knew him very well. She saw the special attention, the glances he gave Lindsey, which he had never given to any other woman

Mary had great respect for Elliot, as a doctor as well as a person. She was surprised at his infatuation with Lindsey, knowing he had a good relationship with Ruth. She thought Elliot, like many other doctors in the hospital, had been going through a midlife crisis. In her estimation, he would end up staying with Ruth. Mary mused to herself that Ruth was such a proper and mannered woman and probably was not giving him the sexual excitement that Lindsey seemed to project. It might be that routine had taken the fun out of the excitement Lindsey was willing to provide. She did not tell Elliot she suspected his affair with Lindsey nor did she tell him that she elected not to tell the police that she suspected the affair. She did not want to make trouble for Elliot with the police or with Ruth.

Elliot rushed to his office, closing the office door behind him, still feeling Mary's eyes peering at his back. *She knows something. She doesn't miss a beat.*

The smiling pictures of Ruth and his children on his desk glared at him. *What in hell was I thinking? Why did I ever accept Lindsey's invitation to visit her gallery? I knew she would try to seduce me.* He saw the reflection of his face in the glass of the picture frames. *She wanted it too. I was completely to blame.*

He remembered that crucial day when he visited the gallery. Ruth was in upstate New York spending a few days at a health spa in the Catskills. Elliot thought it was a good time to take Lindsey up on her invitation. He arrived in the early evening. Her NIRVANA GALLERY was easily recognizable by its elaborate colorful sign on top of the front window. He entered a gallery teeming with browsers and a collection of unique artwork and furniture. The walls were covered with small, intricate oriental carpets, vibrant pictures and wooden sculptures. Everything was displayed with charm and harmony, accented warmly by the expert lighting. Lindsey spotted him through the crowd, smiled, and welcomed him at the door. "Come in, I'm so glad you made it."

"What an amazing place," Elliot said, still trying to take in the overwhelming artwork. Lindsey looked superb in a tight blue leather mini skirt with a red silk shirt that revealed open and wide cleavage. She wore her hair down freely, with a few small strands braided with silver beads to one side.

Lindsey glanced at Elliot and noticed his shyness. *He looks handsome in his elegant suit,* she noticed with satisfaction. Holding his arm, she led him inside. "Let me show you what I do in my free time, Dr. Barrett."

Lindsey pointed to a large elaborately carved wooden table. "This piece is from Bali. Several years ago I spent three months living on that heavenly island and since then I spend some time there every year." Elliot enjoyed Lindsey's enthusiasm and felt entranced by her world. "Most Balinese are originally from India and still practice the Hindu culture and religious life," she continued. "Practically the whole island is devoted to art, and their religion is intertwined with their way of life. For generations they have cultivated the arts in every detail of their daily life in music, dancing, food, architecture and the visual arts. The temples, festivals and offerings are ubiquitous." She paused for a minute, observing Elliot. "Are you interested in all this?"

"Of course, of course. This is fascinating. Please continue."

"The traditional Far Eastern artists were all spiritual people. Their main aims were to express the divine and the picture of the larger reality through their art."

She moved to another section of the gallery. "This painting is from Japan. I like the simple design and discipline. The Zen masters of Japan were influenced by their Buddhist religion and appreciated gentle grace, love of nature, beauty and acute attentiveness. Their long militant samurai tradition integrated with their sense of order and control was imprinted on their society."

Elliot watched with increased interest as Lindsey went from piece to piece and talked about its significance in terms of culture, symbolism, balance and harmony and technique. She stopped next to a wooden Indian carving of Angi the Fire God and explained that the two-headed figure signified the inner and outer fire. "Fire is associated with erotic love in many ancient mythologies," Lindsey explained. "In Tantric teaching throughout the east, sexuality has long been regarded as both an art and a science worthy of study and practice."

"From the little I understand about eastern religion, I thought that sexual power was meant as a tool for liberation and for the desire to transcend the limit of the self. To give as well as to take," suggested Elliot.

"Very good, Elliot. I'm impressed, but I reserve my own interpretation and I use what I want for my gain. The more fascinating pieces are in my personal collection on the second and third floors," Lindsey said as she gently led Elliot to her living quarters. With a word to her assistant to watch the gallery, they climbed up a brown wooden staircase. The apartment was decorated in a style that Elliot had never seen before: a mixture of simplicity, rich colors and fascinating art displayed with great care throughout the space. "The mood and philosophy is determined by the principle and discipline of Zen," she said. "The main idea is for the setting and white walls to punctuate and enhance the art."

Lindsey walked into the bar alcove and opened a bottle of red wine. "It's from Chile, a great wine. You must have a taste."

Elliot examined the bottle of wine with wonder. "Almaviva, 1990 Cabernet-Merlot, by Conche y Toro's? This is new to me."

"They are collaborating with the French to produce magnificent rich wine with subtle, changing flavors. This wine is equivalent to the French's *grand cru classe* Bordeaux," Lindsey said.

"I love wine; we have a long tradition of drinking quality wine in my family. You should see the wine cellar we have in my house and a whole basement full in my parent's house in Boston."

Lindsey poured him wine in a crystal glass.

"Really marvelous. Some of the best I've ever tasted," Elliot said, swirling the glass and enjoying its color, texture and taste.

"Cheers. Always a pleasure to share wine with a person that can appreciate its good quality." She toasted. "Especially with you, Elliot."

"The pleasure is mine. This evening, the art, and your explanations, have all been fascinating. What about this piece of art?" Elliot changed the focus of the conversation, uneasy at being alone with Lindsey.

"She is Kali, the female character of Hinduism. She symbolizes the destructive and creative forces of the universe," Lindsey pointed to the elaborate painting of a female figure with four arms, sitting in a meditative position. "I strongly identify with her attributes."

They sat down on the softly textured white wool sofa. Elliot enjoyed the slight after-taste of the high quality wine. The atmosphere of the dim Japanese lantern lighting, the surrounding colors and the fine Chilean wine relaxed him and awakened his sensuality. When he looked at Lindsey, as if reading his mind, she put on a C.D. of soothing Eastern string music. She remained standing and started moving slowly and sensually in a slow flowing dance. "This feels great," she whispered. Her body moved gracefully as her face expressed a dreamlike joy. Elliot enjoyed watching her movements as he poured himself another glass of wine. He sipped the wine which warmed his throat, and quickened his heartbeat.

Lindsey came over and held his hand, while continuing her dance movements. She whispered, "Let's dance, Elliot. Please dance with me." Elliot felt his inhibitions melt away, and let his body follow the rhythm. Lindsey held his hand and gently placed it on her waist. The warm touch of her body and her perfumed scent intoxicated him. She moved closer to him. Soon they were in each other arms, moving together in unison. She put her head on his shoulder and gently kissed his neck. Warning flashed through Elliot's mind, but he was captivated by the intensity of the moment. Elliot looked in her eyes and kissed her, feeling the warmth of her mouth and the taste of the wine. He searched for her tongue and was delighted with the playful response. Caressing each other, they danced slowly to the rhythm of the music.

Lindsey loosened Elliot's tie, took off his sport coat and placed it on a chair. In a surprising yet natural move she slowly removed her own clothing, revealing a strikingly beautiful body. To his surprise, she did not wear any bra or underpants. Her breasts were perfectly proportioned, and her long legs and flat stomach gave her body a goddess-like quality, like one of her sculptures.

She led him to her bedroom. The cherry wood bed was low to the ground with a silk carpet placed in perfect proportion on the wood floor. The room had very little furniture. She lit the candles above her bed and slowly removed the rest of Elliot's clothing, while leading him to the bed. She looked pleased at Elliot's firm body and delighted at the slight shyness that added to his charm. Lindsey knew how to stroke his body lightly with just the right pressure. Elliot closed his eyes and felt her hands moving over him, skipping his genital area. She traced his stomach and thighs as he felt his body burn with desire.

"Stop teasing me," he pleaded.

"Shhh, no talking allowed." She whispered close to his ear, her warm tongue penetrating his ear cavity, sending pleasure throughout his body. She moved her hands with stronger strokes, passing closer to his genitals, gently stroking his buttocks with her long nails.

Elliot felt his erection on the verge of exploding. He responded by massaging her soft warm skin. She moaned in response to his firm touch and silently directed him to the area that excited her most. Finally, Lindsey slid her body over him as if to continue her dance movements, while sensually rubbing their chests together.

Lindsey knew how to prolong their pleasure by pressing her finger on the base of his penis to stop the flow that was about to set off. When Elliot could not take it any longer he forced his body on top of hers and with strong fast strokes he cried and moaned as he exploded into her.

Lindsey knew how to time her own pleasure and had arched her back in response to the rhythm and climaxed with him.

"I have never felt like this," Elliot said, when he finally managed to catch his breath. "You...you know, you're a real expert in bed."

She cuddled her body against him and sighed in response. In just a few minutes, she felt his body begin to tense.

"I must go," he said abruptly, as if awakening from a fantasy.

Lindsey recognized his response. She had been in relationships with married men before. The sense of guilt was almost automatic after sex. She eased the tension by using her soft relaxing voice. "Would you like to bathe before you go?"

"Yes, that's a good idea," Elliot convinced himself that a little more pleasure would not hurt.

Lindsey took him around a curved glass block wall into a wooden square Japanese bath already filled with hot water. She brought the bottle of wine and entered the bath with him. "Want some more wine?"

"No, I still need to drive across town," he said, suddenly eager to bring the night to a close.

"You can stay over here."

Although Ruth was not home, he could not imagine himself staying the whole night. "No. Really, I must go."

They bathed together playfully, but he knew the perfect evening was coming to an end.

7

"George, what's up? My secretary told me you called," Ted said on the phone.

"Oh yeah, give me a minute to find the file in all this mess. It's about the Dr. Elliot Barrett case. There it is."

"What about it?"

"Well, I called to tell you that the coroner has finished his report and the police wrapped up the investigation. I'm afraid your client is in deep shit. All the evidence is pointing in his direction."

"What have you got there, George?"

"It's too long of a report to go into on the phone. I'll send over a courier today, with the entire discovery for you to look over, and then we'll talk again."

"I'll be waiting for it."

"I'll get it there by noon."

"Thanks, George."

Ted recalled his meeting with Elliot the day before to discuss what he had gathered so far about the case. He wanted to find out all he could from Elliot about the exact nature of his relationship with Lindsey, and about the physical evidence found in Lindsey's, apartment. Elliot held his position as before, denying any wrongdoing. Ted explained that the D.A.'s office is processing the case and that in a few days he would be hearing from George.

The package arrived by courier. Ted closed the door and told Melissa he did not want to be disturbed. He looked at the discovery package for a long time. Finally he gathered the courage to open it. He quickly scanned the two reports, that of the first officer on the scene and that of the detective signed to take over the investigation. When he got to the photographs, he felt his stomach turn upside down. He had to pause and take a long deep breath. Seeing Lindsey's dead body on the couch sent spasms through his body and produced a sharp pain in his chest.

The events of that dreadful night flashed vividly through his mind. Ted had called Lindsey's gallery on the morning of her death. "Lindsey I want to tell you something very important. I'm free tonight and I'm going to come over around 8:30 P.M." Ted had been excited to share his surprise with her.

"Why aren't you asking me if it's a good time for me too?" Lindsey asked.

Ted was taken aback. "I'm sorry, my beauty. Just too excited with my news.

May I ...?"

"Okay, okay but what is all this surprise?"

"I want to keep the surprise until I see you tonight," Ted said, trying to retain his charming voice. "Can you make one of your gourmet dinners for us?"

"I won't be able to; I'll be busy throughout the day."

Ted tried to contain his disappointment. He wanted to create a special event when telling her what he had been thinking about for the last few weeks. "Never mind. I'll pick up Thai food," Ted said, not letting any obstacles ruin his plan.

"I got to go, I'll see you around 8:30," Lindsey said.

Ted rubbed her the wrong way sometimes, but he excited her. In many ways she liked his aggression, but also felt repulsed by his obsessive need to control. Elliot was gentle and soft-spoken. In some ways he lacked the spice that stimulated her, yet she found security in his solid and orderly nature. *Would that they were both one man. But I can settle for both and get what I need.*

With Ted, Lindsey enjoyed going out on the town and letting the mood dictate the night, without censor. With Elliot, she liked going to dinner and having long conversations on stimulating subjects. Lindsey enjoyed the sustained, passionate sex with Elliot and the wild, uncontrollable sex with Ted. With Elliot she fulfilled the need of being with someone that gave her what her father had not provided, and with Ted she felt she was allowed to be a child again.

Ted left his apartment that night, not feeling any need to tell Heather where he was going. He knew they would not remain together much longer. Their relationship had come to a standstill, with no sign of improvement. She had tried to get pregnant, but refused the doctor's recommendation for infertility treatment. She feared the ill effects the treatment might cause her body. He just didn't care. They had been drifting apart for the last few years to the point where days might pass without saying a word to each other.

Ted spent the last few months rearranging his financial accounts to disguise his real wealth. He regretted he had not thought of a prenuptial agreement that would have saved him a lot of money. *Makes me sick that I have worked my ass off for my money, and might have to share it with a woman who hardly does anything all day.* He knew he could not hide all his money, but managed to conceal much of it.

He drove down Broadway past the theater district watching the flood of people weaving between restaurants and Broadway shows. Stopping at a florist shop, he bought the largest flower bouquet the merchant offered. He passed the neon canyon lights of Time Square, a glorious dipole crackling with excitement and energy. He stopped in to pick up the Thai food and went next door to the liqueur store to purchase a good bottle of wine. Then, continued driving to south SoHo and took a right turn on Prince Street.

Ted didn't want to be late and looking for a parking spot in Manhattan was always a daunting task. Prince was a one-way traffic street, and he didn't want to time going around the block. He finally found an illegal parking spot between two buildings next to a garbage dump, not caring if he got a parking ticket. Ted showed up exactly on time at Lindsey's door.

He rang the bell a few times and waited apprehensively until Lindsey finally opened the door. She was wearing a bathrobe.

"What beautiful flowers," she said. "Give me just a minute or two to get dressed. You can put the flowers in the vase on the counter for me." Disappearing up the staircase, she said over her shoulder, "Will you open a bottle of white wine? You know where it is."

Ted set the flowers in the vase, poured the wine and pressed the C.D. button. Then he sat back and closed his eyes, delighted with the mellow jazz trumpet of Miles Davis.

Perfect, he thought rubbing his hands together. *Just the right mood.*

To Ted's disappointment, Lindsey came down casually dressed, wearing no shoes and no makeup. "I love the flowers," she said. "But one of these days I need to teach you how they should be set." She moved the vase back to the way it had been. "It must be placed in harmony with the rest of the surroundings. Flowers should be arranged with more care." She took a long moment to attentively observe the variety, and then with skillful hands arranged the flowers, stepping back and forth until she felt the arrangement was just right. "Now they are perfect. Thanks for the flowers."

Ted usually liked to be in control of any situation. He did not like when Lindsey tried to teach him, as if he was incompetent but chose not to respond. Tonight he had different ideas in mind.

"Come sit next to me," Ted said. He held her hand and looked directly into her eyes. "I've waited all day for this moment." He pulled a velvet box out of his pocket and gave it to Lindsey.

Lindsey opened the box, astonished. "What a beautiful bracelet! What is the occasion?"

"Do you like it?"

"It's beautiful, the jade is gorgeous."

Ted looked in Lindsey eyes, as her placed the bracelet on her wrist and chose his words carefully. "I have been carrying it with me for a week. This is only part of the surprise."

Lindsey gave Ted a passionate kiss. "I love it. It's really beautiful."

Ted looked at Lindsey with satisfaction. "Listen Lindsey, we have been seeing each other for the last six months. I've fallen in love with you."

Lindsey laughed lightly. "You are a married man, Ted."

"I've been thinking about it a lot. You are the most fun and amazing woman I have ever met. This is what I wanted to surprise you about. I'm planning to divorce Heather."

Lindsey was indeed surprised. She got up to pour another glass of wine. "Ted... I'm flattered ... but you should know me by now. I am not interested in an exclusive relationship."

"What are you saying? I'm willing to get divorced and be only with you. I thought you would love the idea."

"Love the idea? I did not say or do anything to make you believe that."

Ted was agitated. His plan had fallen flat. "Isn't it every woman's dream to find herself with one man?"

Lindsey giggled. "You are really silly. I have no such dream, never have. I own myself. I don't want to be limited to a monogamous relationship."

Ted hated the fact she was taking everything he said so lightly. "What are you saying?"

"Maybe I did not make myself clear in the past. Look Ted, just like you have a relationship going on with your wife, I have a relationship with another man."

"Another man! Why didn't you tell me?" Ted shouted.

"I don't owe you reports! Some aspects of my life I don't feel like sharing."

"What do you call what we have together?" Ted's face turned red. She tried to calm him, to reason with him.

"What we have between us is exclusive to us. The rest of my life is mine. What do we have? Passionate quickies, good fucks, good dinners, lots of fun and great times. I hope I'm speaking for both of us."

Ted got hold of himself and decided to reveal his vulnerability. "Come here, please. Sit next to me," he said softly, as he waited for her to come to him. "That sounds very cold. What about feelings?"

"I don't know about you, but for me the only feelings I'm willing to discuss are what we have between us, not feelings I have with others."

"What others? Who are you talking about? Who is he?"

"I never discuss other relationships, but this night I will make an exception so everything will be cleared up and this subject will not come up again."

Ted was furious, but he needed to hear what she had to say.

"I have developed a close relationship with another man."

"Are you fucking him …?" Ted yelled, losing his cool again.

"I don't think that's any of your business," she snapped back, moving farther away from him.

"If you must know, he's a nice doctor who is married just like you. We have the same understanding."

"A doctor? Do I know him?"

"No, I don't think so. He's been taking care of my mother at the Cancer Center Hospital."

"Cancer Center, I know people from there. Who is he?"

"Dr. Elliot Barrett. That shouldn't mean anything to you." Lindsey disclosed Elliot's name in the heat of the moment and immediately realized her mistake. She always regretted being dragged into this kind of discussion. "Listen Ted. That's all you get from me. I'm not on trial and you are not cross examining me."

Ted jumped up as if he had been bitten by a snake. He couldn't control his anger. *Elliot, I cannot believe that bastard*, he thought. *Elliot, that son of a bitch always has everything fall into his lap.* Years of stored jealousy rose to the surface of his mind. He grabbed Lindsey's hands tightly. "What is this? Some kind of mind game? You cannot play with people like this."

Lindsey got up, trying to detach her hands from Ted's grip. "Let go of my hands," she yelled, furiously trying to release her hands from Ted's strong grip. "Let me go, let go of my hands!" Her rage grew as she desperately tried to pull away her hands. "Who do you think you are? What about you? This is your second divorce," she screamed. "You're thinking of making me your third wife. What do you call that…?"

Ted's anger turned to rage. "You are some kind of heartless bitch. I don't need you." Ted suddenly released his grip. Lindsey, her eyes wide with surprise, lost her sense of balance and tripped falling backwards, hitting a chair. She fell to the side and hit the back of her head on the corner of the wooden couch. She lost her breath and consciousness.

Ted was horrified by the sight of Lindsey tripping backward and tried desperately to move forward to capture her, but the chair was in his way. He heard the hollow sound of her skull hitting the wood. Ted rushed toward Lindsey, almost tripping over the broken chair. When he saw that she was not breathing, he panicked.

"I killed her!" he said frantically. "I killed her!"

His first instinct was to run toward the door but he got hold of himself. He came back, stood still for a moment to clear his mind, and decided what course of action to take. He took the bottle of wine, the food he brought and wiped all the places his fingers might have left their prints. Then, looking around to see if he left any evidence, he remembered the bracelet. Ted removed the bracelet from Lindsey's wrist. Remembering the flowers, he stuffed them in a paper bag. Arms full, he carefully closed the door and disappeared into the dark alley, not seeing the pair of eyes watching from inside a big cardboard box.

8

A mood of elation in the District Attorney's office: George and his staff had gathered to watch the Mayor speak on television. The day before, encouraging crime statistics had been published in the Times. The crime rate had plunged considerably. This year it went down an amazing twenty-two percent. In his speech the Mayor thanked everyone involved in the accomplishment, among them the law enforcement officers on the streets and the District Attorney's office.

The office staff stood up clapping and high-fiving one another while smiling with satisfaction. Their hard work had finally paid off. "Shhh everybody, let's listen." George sat glued to the television screen as the press began asking questions. "What about the danger that City Hall will pressure law enforcement to quickly reduce crime, giving too much power to the police?" one reporter asked.

"Before I came to this office," the Mayor responded, "the crime rate in this city was continuously rising and criminals controlled the streets. It affected tourism, commerce, and consequently the economic welfare of the city, not to mention the reduction in the quality of life of our citizens. In my campaign I promised that we would stop it. And stop it we did."

"You are not addressing the issue of …" the reporter insisted.

"Excuse me, I am answering," the Mayor interrupted. "The demand of the people at the grassroots level was to be tough on criminals. The era of the policy of the revolving door where criminals were once being released before their sentence was completed, is over. We are taking back the streets."

"You're damn right!" one of the assistants, Sharon Diller, shouted.

"Will everybody sit down and listen?" George pleaded. He knew the questioner addressed an important issue. *The consciousness in this country has been swinging like a pendulum*, he thought. *The pendulum has shifted in the past from less individual rights to more police power, and back and forth. With more pressure on the system to arrest and convict criminals there is a danger that it will be at the cost of individual rights. More innocent individuals will fall victim to the system. That is the nature of the American justice system, and it is probably the best in the world.* He looked around the office and then back to the television press conference.

George's concern was confirmed when the television reporter interviewed people on the street for their comments. "Out with the liberals!" one merchant yelled, "We will not let them destroy our country." A well-dressed woman added, "Three strikes and you're out." Assuming an expression of importance on her face, she added, "Lock them up and throw away the key. That's what needs to be done."

I must be sensitive to this issue and not fall prey to all this euphoria and mass hysteria, George concluded.

Ted watched the mayor's press conference in his office. He realized this mood on the street would pose challenges for lawyers and affect judges and the juries. On the other hand, it may create more business.

He picked up the phone and called George. "What do you think about the mayor's performance?"

"It's all politics. They are feeding the masses with a bunch of hogwash," George muttered.

"You can't argue with numbers and statistics and definitely not with police success," Ted said.

"Hey forget about that. Did you go through the discovery I sent you?"

"Sure did buddy, and you don't have much there. It's all circumstantial."

"We don't agree. There is plenty of evidence to convict. We've decided to take it to the grand jury."

"I see. Why don't we meet tomorrow and arrange our schedules," Ted said.

"Come over at one o'clock and we'll have lunch together," George said.

"You're on for lunch tomorrow." Ted hung up the telephone. *The trap is set and the prey will take the bait,* he thought sarcastically. *Elliot is thinking he is already off the hook.*

The next day during lunch George outlined for Ted the reasons for his decision to take the case to the grand jury. "We're willing to go with second degree murder. It seems like a crime of passion. No drugs, no weapons, no forced entry."

"I don't buy that theory. It will be even harder to convince a jury."

"Look Ted, you know we can drag it out in court or we can… listen Ted, I'm in the mood for a good deal. Take advantage of the situation for your client and let's come up with a plea bargain and finish with it."

"What are you proposing?"

"Involuntary manslaughter, five years, low-security prison. With good behavior he will be out in three years and Dr. Barrett can go back to his life," George said.

"A very good offer if Dr. Barrett is guilty. But he maintains he is not!"

George had difficulty trying to read Ted's mind. *Is he playing hard ball or really ready for a fight in court?* "Come on Ted. They all say they're innocent," he said with a dismissing hand gesture. "You know it's better for your client to deal now rather than later. Give him the proposal and you'll see Dr. Barrett grab the deal. Tell him that trial is a much riskier proposition."

"You haven't even presented the case to the grand jury."

"A detail. We certainly can establish that they were lovers. From there it's easy. You know, a married man, respected, afraid of scandal. We can make it fit like a glove."

"You remember what happened with the unfitted glove?" Ted teased.

"O.J., it just doesn't fit," George laughed. "We both know that was a fiasco. Let's be serious. In this case we have a preponderance of evidence to tie him to the crime."

"Give me a few days to get back to you. I need to give the offer to Dr. Barrett. I don't think he'll go for it."

"Do that, and also tell him that if we drag it into court we won't be so generous."

George noticed that Ted was not as feisty during lunch as on previous cases. *Is that a new tactic? I can't make out what's going on in Ted's mind.*

Having driven back to his office, he received pages of telephone messages from his secretary. "Dr. Barrett already called twice this morning. He left a message to call him as soon as you get back from the meeting."

"Thanks. They're going to the grand jury with his case. Get him on my office phone."

Ted looked out of his office window at the rain pouring down on the rooftops of Manhattan's crowded skyline. The Statue of Liberty was barely visible as it blended with the gray reflection on the water below and the dark clouds. *It would be so perfect,* he thought, *if Elliot accepts the plea bargain. Everything will be over. Elliot will suffer a bit just like I suffered and we will be even. Justice will be served.*

Elliot had come out exhausted from a three-hour surgery case. During surgery, he could concentrate on the task at hand and the fast action and forget about the outside world. The call from Ted's office forced him back into his grim reality. "Ted, what's the news?"

"When can you come to my office today?" Ted asked.

"Is it bad?"

"We need to discuss some options."

"I can be there in twenty minutes."

As he drove to Ted's office, Elliot was nervous about the outcome of the meeting. He almost hit a car that emerged out of his blind spot and was cursed out by the driver. He almost turned on a one-way street, retreating only when the angry horns warned him of his mistake. By the time he reached Ted's office the rain was coming down hard. He was soaking wet when he met Ted.

You're soaking wet, take off your coat."

"So, what happened?" Elliot said even before taking his coat off.

"I'm sorry, but they are planning to ask the grand jury for an indictment."

"Grand jury? But you ... I thought you could avoid that. "

"It's completely their decision. Of course I argued, but in the end it's the D.A.'s internal politics that matter."

Elliot was shivering from the cold rain and bad news.

Ted chose his words carefully. "As your lawyer, I also have to tell you that George feels he has plenty of evidence against you. He proposed a plea bargain."

"A plea bargain?" Elliot sunk down in the chair as he saw his world collapsing in front of his eyes. He had been hoping Ted could somehow eradicate his problem. Now his case would be in the public record for all to see. His face showed his strain and agony.

"This is only for your consideration," Ted explained. "I'm just conveying George's proposal. It's my duty as your lawyer."

"To accept the plea would mean having to say I did it. I'm not willing to do that."

"I knew you would say that and I told George that would be your response. But again, as your lawyer, I need to tell you that they will go all the way if you refuse. They will ask for the full penalty."

"You couldn't convince them that I'm innocent?" Elliot asked in desperation.

"I can contend anything, but in the end it's their decision. George says he can prove you were lovers and then ..."

"I am telling you, Ted. It was only a doctor-patient relationship."

"Look Elliot, they believe differently. They found your fingerprints all over the place, plus hair samples. We are going to argue, of course, but in the end it's what the jury wants to believe."

"You mean they can convict an innocent man?" Elliot tried desperately to hold his position, and Ted was astonished at Elliot's ability to lie in such a convincing manner. He felt the urge to tell Elliot he knew he had an affair with Lindsey, but he could never disclose how and why he knew. "I did not say I will let them believe that. That's why I am here," Ted said. "All I can do now is giving you all the facts, so that you will be informed."

"Are you saying, I should take the offer?"

"First of all, I did not say any such thing. It is completely your decision." Ted thought fast and decided it was the right time to push the issue further. He hoped to end it all by convincing Elliot to accept the plea. "If you choose to go that route," Ted said delicately, "we have some bargaining room to counter offer. I think we might be able to get a better deal."

"I will not accept any deal. I didn't do anything." Elliot's face showed all the horror of what he was thinking. "Everything would be exposed for all to see. Dragging me to court would provide public information. What of my clinic, my wife, my family?"

"At this point, there's not much we can do," Ted said. "The New York Superior Court would order jurors to serve, supposedly composed of objective observers. Remember that in grand jury hearings only the prosecutors can call witnesses."

"What if you can convince the grand jury I am innocent?"

Ted decided to release the pressure. "That's exactly what I intend to do. Plea bargaining can be offered and accepted on a later date. I am going to talk to the judge and to George and request a pretrial preliminary hearing instead of a grand jury."

"What's the difference?"

"It's to your advantage. The grand jury could indict a ham sandwich," Ted tried to ease the tension.

"Ham sandwich? What are you talking about?"

"It's legal jargon. It means that the D. A. can get the grand jury to indict pretty much anyone."

"What about you?"

"I can't even be there. George can manipulate the jury to basically do what he wants them to do. On the other hand, in the preliminary hearing the prosecutor has to work harder to show a strong suspicion that the crime was committed by you. I can also question the witnesses and get a better opportunity to test the D.A.'s trial plan to see how their witnesses do under my cross examination. This is a circumstantial case. I know I can cause the D.A. to lose his enthusiasm; we can dismiss the whole case and avoid the trial."

"Who makes the final decision to take me to trial?"

"A neutral officer of the court. In this case, a judge can determine if the state has enough evidence to proceed against you."

Elliot was filled with hope. "I know you can do it Ted. You're a great lawyer."

Stop kissing ass when you're desperate, Ted thought. *You have no idea what kind of a good lawyer I am and this case is my masterpiece. You don't even know that a hearing would create more exposure than a Grand Jury.* Ted looked at Elliot with pity.

"This is only the first phase. At the end we will be victorious," he said—meaning, "I will be victorious."

9

Ted made a motion to dismiss the case through a pretrial preliminary hearing.

The court judge established that the proceedings would start on December 2nd, the first Monday after Thanksgiving. Ted had been closely following the progress of the investigation and was studying the discovery. He was hoping that at some point he would manage to convince Elliot that a plea bargain would be the less risky option, but at least to give the appearance of providing proper counsel.

He couldn't help feeling a bit sorry for what he was doing to Elliot. He didn't want Elliot to suffer too much or be incarcerated for too long; he felt ambivalent. On the one hand, he liked and admired Elliot and cherished their friendship. On the other hand, he had a long history of resentment and jealousy that he had repressed throughout the years of their friendship.

When they were still students, Elliot took Ted to visit his parents' estate in Massachusetts. Ted remembered his shock when they arrived at gates leading to vast manicured gardens with tall trees in front of a huge stone mansion. The butler opened the massive front doors and Ted was led into a home and lifestyle he had never experienced. The grand entry foyer floor was covered with Italian marble, which led to a split set of curved staircases. The living room had large classical-style original paintings on the walls. The tall wood-stained ceilings held massive crystal chandeliers. The furniture was of the same classical style and rested over a thick oriental carpet. Arched windows opened to a large backyard with a pool that almost seemed to border the ocean.

A servant brought their suitcases to the upper level of the mansion. Ted's guest room was adjacent to Elliot's. When he entered Elliot's room he couldn't believe his eyes. The windows were opened to a spectacular ocean view. His king-size bed looked small in proportion to the space. Against the wall was a large built-in entertainment center with a flat-screen TV. When he entered Elliot's walk-in closet he thought he was in a clothing shop. The enormous room had rows of clothes hanging neatly on all four walls. In the center was a built-in island of dressers with a thick marble slab top.

Ted's astonishment was mixed with envy. He could not understand why one person could have all the possessions in the world and another could be born into poverty. The pain of envy was now exposed, although he felt he had no right to feel that way. This hidden bitterness lurked, ready to spring whenever he was in similar situations.

Ted came from a working-class family and grew up in a small house a few miles from downtown Detroit. Those who could afford to moved out of the neighborhood and poorer families replaced them. The municipal government didn't invest its resources there, and the neighborhood became an unpleasant place to live. His two older brothers followed their father's footsteps and worked in the auto industry on an assembly line. His two sisters married into the same fate.

Ted instinctively knew that the only way out of this cycle of poverty was through education. As soon as Ted started to make money, he managed to move his parents to a better neighborhood in Dearborn. Periodically, he sent them money that dwarfed their small social security checks. A few years after retirement, his father's health deteriorated; he died within a year. Ted moved his mother to a nice retirement center and occasionally he went to visit her there.

Throughout the years of their friendship, Ted's resentment surfaced and was repressed over and over again. He convinced himself that, with unrelenting effort, he would one day reach Elliot's financial position. His success and wealth were already considerable but not yet close to Elliot's. A few of his investments proved to be fruitful, and his reputation as a great lawyer had yielded status as well as great financial gain. It seemed however that there was always a lurking fear that one day he would lose it all. There was a sense of inner emptiness that was covered by layers of unrelenting ambition that kept him in constant movement to fill that void.

Living with Elliot as undergraduates was a financial burden as Ted tried to keep up with his share of the bills. He saw Elliot use his credit card without needing to put any thought into what he was spending. Elliot used his vacation time to travel with his parents and always came back tan and refreshed for the next semester. Ted had to work a few days a week as well as on weekends during the school year. Also he worked full time on his vacations in a five-star restaurant on Fifth Avenue. In one meal his wealthy customers would spend what it took him a month to earn as a waiter. He learned quickly that by being charming, he could convince the patrons to accept his recommendations to purchase the more expensive food and wine. He learned how to delight the ladies and charm them with his wittiness. Often his tips exceeded the customary percentage Ted loved women and was intoxicated by their beauty, their scent, and their sensuous figures. Their presence energized him. He believed he could read their minds and give them exactly what they wanted. Ted learned quickly that money and power were desired commodities and he grew more and more determined to obtain them. He was not afraid to take a risk by approaching a woman and asking for her telephone number. For Ted, the intense game of hunting and conquering was better than the relationship itself. He did not have long-term relationships. Often they ended with bitter, hurt feelings.

Elliot's luck with women was another source of envy for Ted. Women would approach Elliot and make advances toward him. He did not have to make any effort to attract them. When he found a woman he liked, he felt committed to the relationship until it ended naturally. Ted attracted women who were very different from those drawn to Elliot. Elliot found Ted's type to be shallow and, in many cases, superficial.

Melissa, Ted's secretary, entered his office and placed the Post on his desk. "I thought you might be interested," she said. There was a short article stating that the investigation of the death of Lindsey Anderson had been completed. The police had ruled out suicide, and a preliminary hearing was scheduled to convene on the second of December for the hearing of Dr. Elliot Barrett. The district attorney's office believes they have probable cause to go before the hearing and to indict on voluntary manslaughter.

Ted was surprised at the small exposure the murder case received. Scanning the headlines, he realized Elliot's good luck. *That son of a gun, Elliot*, he thought smiling, *there is so much pressing news today that his story was pushed to the back of the paper.*

Ted telephoned Elliot to get his reaction. "Hi Elliot, did you see the article?"

"Five minutes ago. What an embarrassment."

"It'll get very little notice."

"Hopefully."

"Forget it. Let's get together for a game of racquetball this evening."

"I haven't had the desire to do anything but work since this mess started."

Melissa entered the room and told Ted there was an urgent call from Ruth on the other line. "Elliot, stay on the line for a minute. Ruth is on the other line…" Ted pressed the button, connecting Ruth. "What a coincidence, Ruth. Elliot is on the other line."

"Ted, the police are here and they want to search the house," Ruth said with a shrieking voice.

"Did they show you a search warrant?"

"Yes. What should I do?"

"You must let them in. I'll be there shortly and I'll tell Elliot to join us." Ruth watched with shame as three policemen and a detective entered the house.

"My name is Detective Benjamin Sills," the detective said. He explained to her what they intended to do. He was polite and apologized for the inconvenience, but he seemed very determined. They started their search on the top floor and went from room to room. They opened all the drawers and closets, emptying everything out and leaving it in disarray.

Ruth felt that her only sanctuary and privacy—her home—was being severely violated. She kept her tears from falling, badly wanting to keep her dignity, the little shred that was still left untouched. They glanced at her, pretending they did not notice her, as she followed them around her house. She could sense their quick glances and ironic smiles as they noticed all the signs of wealth. They took their time inspecting Elliot's office.

The front door opened and Elliot came in the house, with inner torment clearly visible on his face. Ruth ran to him and they hugged each other, sharing the disheartening situation. "Has Ted arrived?" Elliot said.

"No, but what can he do?"

Elliot looked up and saw Detective Sills entering his office. He and Ruth felt the same way when Ted arrived, hoping he could save them from this distressing situation. Ted took charge and, with his assertive demeanor, restored their fragile confidence. He spoke to Sills, making sure the search warrant was signed and legally obtained. When the cops questioned Ruth, he made sure they didn't violate any of her rights.

"I need to inspect the content of the safe." Detective Sills said as he left Elliot's office.

Elliot hesitantly looked at Ted for instruction. He reluctantly opened the safe after Ted nodded approval. Elliot and Ruth felt violated as Detective Sills started empting the content of the safe.

Ted looked with envy as the large collection of jewelry that spilled out over Elliot's desk. There were large carats diamonds of rings necklaces, pins and bracelets, large precious stones embedded in ornate antique gold. Jewelry that was given to Ruth by her family, and Elliot's family and jewelry that Elliot had purchased throughout the years of their marriage.

"Is all this necessary?" Ruth muttered, uncomfortable with the wealth being displayed before the detectives. She noticed Ted's captivated stare and felt even more embarrassed.

Ted took hold of the awkward situation with an apologetic gesture, acknowledging Sills' explanation for the necessary search. Methodically, the detective continued pulling out piles of stock and bonds and large amounts of cash as he dictated to his assistant the description of the contact.

It took the policemen another hour to finish their search. "They seem to be leaving empty-handed," Ted said when they finally left.

"There is nothing they could find," Elliot said, feeling guilty that Ruth had to endure such a situation. Ted explained how he managed to arrange a preliminary hearing instead of the grand jury. They sat for a while at the kitchen table drinking coffee and discussing the case.

"Elliot, listen. The search is over, so how about changing the scenery for a game of racquetball?"

"I don't know, Ted."

"It will be good for you, you need it. It will release some of the pressure."

"He's right, Elliot," Ruth said. "Why not? I'll tidy up."

"Okay," Elliot said reluctantly.

"How about 8:30 tonight?" Ted almost retreated when he said 8:30, remembering it was the time he had asked to come to Lindsey's, on the night of her death.

"8:30 is fine," Elliot said as Ted left to return to his office.

Later that evening at the gym, Ted looked at himself in the dressing room mirror.

Although he kept up a good work-out routine every week, he had started to develop a little paunch. He was trying to cover his thinning hair on the top by extending the hair from each side. He had bulky legs, too stubby for his liking. He preferred the looks of himself dressed in suits that emphasized his success.

Ted and Elliot had an ongoing bet. The first to win ten games of racquetball would be the victor and pay for a nice dinner. Within the current match Ted had tied the score at nine to nine. One more game would decide the winner. Elliot had introduced the game of racquetball to Ted at college. Ted had gained proficiency until it was close to Elliot's.

After a short warm-up they started their match. The game was close and Elliot showed signs of fatigue faster than usual, but kept up with Ted. In the last game, Ted stretched out his arm as he raced toward the ball bouncing off the wall, desperately trying to catch his breath. Salty sweat rolled down his face, penetrating and burning his eyes, yet it did not deter his resolve. Ted wanted to win this bet so badly. Elliot's longer arms managed to maneuver faster and return the ball with a strong swing. Ted hit it back, and after a few more challenging swings, was able to win the set and match the score. "One more game and your ass is mine," he said, looking proudly at Elliot.

"Taking advantage of a guy when he's down," Elliot smiled, wiping sweat from his face. "Thanks Ted, I didn't realize I needed to exercise so badly. I was a bundle of nerves. It could affect my surgery. I'm more relaxed now. We should get back to doing it more often."

Ted saw the underlying agony on Elliot's face. He could not help feeling a little guilty realizing the severity of the situation. After all, Elliot was being blamed for murder and was already publicly humiliated. He might be incarcerated. One more pressing thought tugged at the back of Ted's mind. *Since I have a personal involvement in this court case, ethically I shouldn't have accepted it.* But he still felt anger towards Elliot for causing him to explode on the night of Lindsey's death.

They went to a coffee shop and sat at a corner booth drinking coffee while they talked about the case. Elliot was debating privately if should he take a chance and raise the issue he had been thinking about. He decided to give it a shot.

"Why shouldn't I take a lie detector test?" Elliot asked. "Why not talk to the police?"

"First of all, lie detector tests are not admissible in a court of law. Secondly, I always advise my clients not to speak to the police. Let them find their own theories."

"But why?" Elliot didn't really want to answer questions, but he knew most innocent people made such an offer.

What is Elliot thinking about? Ted wondered. *He's trying to continue his deception, but he is careful not to seem objectionable.* "What the police often do when they do not have enough evidence," Ted said convincingly, "is question a suspect and then, in court, refute his statements. With my tactic they cannot refute. They have to work harder to dig for evidence. In my experience, in most cases they cannot deliver and they back down."

Ted was surprised that Elliot was not more adamant about insisting on taking the lie detector test if he felt so strongly he was innocent. In his many years as a lawyer he knew when his client was lying. If he didn't know better, he would suspect Elliot was the murderer but Ted attributed it to Elliot's fear that his affair would be exposed. *What a coward. Elliot should face me, Ruth and his family like a man and admit that he failed them and come clean. So he had an affair, it's no big deal.*

But Ted knew better. He knew that he, himself, had left Lindsey dead on the couch.

10

In the days before Thanksgiving, Elliot's family was gloomy. The children flew in from college for the long weekend. They expressed their distress and asked Elliot some hard questions. Elliot decided against going to Boston to see his parents. He didn't want to face their requests for more information. He insisted it was all a mistake and Ted was working to clear him.

Ruth was determined to keep the family united behind Elliot. She worked hard to prepare the food and the house for the holiday. She even surprised Elliot with a suggestion to invite Ted and Heather for dinner. She decided to start viewing Ted from a positive perspective; after all, he has been working very hard for Elliot. Ruth was learning to respect a new side of Ted's character. He called almost daily and kept her and Elliot informed and calm. She appreciated his sensitivity and respected his concern and encouragement. Elliot appreciated the gesture and was happy when Ted agreed to join them for Thanksgiving.

At the dinner, Ruth managed to conceal her own worries. She arranged the table with grace and care, with all the proper arrangements and a colorful flower bouquet as the centerpiece. The large chandelier shed its bright light over the dining room table, and the dishes and silverware sparkled. With her relentless energy, she kept the evening going provoking laughter by telling funny stories. There was an unspoken agreement not to mention the case. Ted felt honored when asked to carve the large turkey. The food was served on beautiful silver trays and as the butler made sure the glasses stayed full.

Ted's wit and humor were charming. He clearly supported

Ruth's intentions to keep everyone calm and united-if not distract-
ed. At one point, he told a touching story about his poor grandpar-
ents who had emigrated from Poland. Although they owned very
little, Thanksgiving meant a great deal to them spiritually. At one
moment he raised his glass for a toast. "I shamefully admit that in
the last years I have forgotten the rich feelings of Thanksgiving
that I just remembered this evening. I'm truly thankful to Elliot
and Ruth for this delightful evening recapturing my sweet forgotten
memories."

Everyone joined in toasting his thoughts.

At the end of the meal Heather joined Ruth in the kitchen.
"Thanks for the invitation," Heather said. "It's so good to celebrate
with your family."

"You're welcome. I'm happy you could make it. We usually go
to Boston to share the evening with Elliot's parents."

"Since I married Ted, I haven't been with a family on holidays.
We usually just do it alone. Ted never wants to go to his family or
mine," she said sadly.

Ruth took notice of Heather's new, lively energy. Heather had
slimmed down and was dressed provocatively for Thanksgiving.
She had breast implants, and her cleavage was exposed. Her hand
dramatically played with her blond bouffant hairstyle. She wore a
beautiful jade bracelet that seemed out of place with the rest of her
outfit and taste. Ruth was aware of her childlike quality, constantly
needing to please and gain approval. Heather's eyes seemed to be
saying, "I'm a victim, I'm weak, please don't hurt me."

"Do you and Ted spend a lot of time together?" Ruth asked.

"To tell you the truth, we didn't use to that much. For a long
time we didn't get along so well, but really, just the last month or so,
he has been completely different."

"Different? What do you mean?"

"You know how charming he can be when he wants to. Almost
as nice as when he was first pursuing me."

"That good, huh? Maybe there's guilt, you know ..." Ruth

laughed, intentionally bumping into Heather's side.

"No. Not like that. You know flowers, good sex," Heather whispered, laughing like a teenager sharing a secret. "He stopped criticizing every little thing I do and stays home much more often. I love that."

"Yes, we're also fortunate that he's working very hard for Elliot. Maybe that also has to do with his renewed energy," Ruth said thankfully.

"I'll tell you a secret. We almost decided to separate right before all this happened. Nothing I did was right. Now it's like a miracle. A hundred-and-eighty degree change. I just want him to continue this way."

"Good. I hope for your sake it all continues. Actually, for both of you." Ruth hugged Heather and felt the unique warmth that two women feel when free to exchange an intimate moment.

When Ted and Heather had left, and the children were downstairs watching television and catching up with each other, Ruth felt satisfied with the successful evening. Exhausted by the long day, she fell asleep quickly. Elliot lay in bed tossing and turning as his thoughts raced. He remembered his father's phone call that morning, trying to convince him one last time to join his family for Thanksgiving. His father was very disappointed when Elliot told him he would not be joining them. *Long overdue to release the emotional and psychological grip I've let my father have over me*, Elliot thought. He felt gratified to have rejected his father's suggestion that a family lawyer participate in his defense.

"Fine," his father replied. "But I plan to have my lawyer follow the court proceedings from Boston. I reserve the option to change your mind if I feel Ted is not doing a good enough job."

"Dad, I would appreciate it if you let me handle my own affairs. You can make suggestions but I make my own decisions."

"What's with you, Elliot? You have never talked like this before."

"I'm forty-eight years old, and I still feel like a child when I talk to you. It's time to make my own choices without you demanding an account."

"You're under stress, Elliot. All we care is for your own good."

"I'm under stress but that's beside the point. Please. Let go of the need to watch over me."

"That's what I said. I'll let my lawyer observe from here. I didn't insist on him being in New York at this point, did I?"

Elliot realized that trying to get the last word in with his father was a losing proposition. He would keep communication at bay for the time being.

The holiday weekend moved slowly. Ruth answered all the telephone calls from friends, and explained with conviction that it was a case of mistaken identity. It spared Elliot the torment of repeating his lie over and over again.

One phone call Ruth was happy to pass on to Elliot was from Margaret, Lindsey's mother. "This is Thanksgiving Day, and I felt compelled to call you. First, I want to thank you for saving my life with your operation and treatment. Secondly, I want to tell you I do not believe anything they have accused you of. I have heard only praise about you from my daughter. I have confidence that you are innocent, and the truth will come to light soon."

Elliot heart's plummeted as he fought to maintain his composure. "Thank you for your kind words. I needed to hear them at this time, especially from you, Margaret. I was so sorry to hear about Lindsey. With all the confusion I've had to face, I haven't even called to offer my condolences. I was very fond of Lindsey. She was a very special person."

"Thanks for your kind words. I'm sure everything will turn out in your favor. Then perhaps they will look for my daughter's killer."

"We'll be in touch," Elliot said.

In answer to Ruth's inquisitive look, Elliot had to pretend that he was touched by Margaret's phone call. Actually, his heart raced and his mind was troubled.

"What did she say?" Ruth asked.

"She said she believes I'm innocent."

"That's good. That will be good for the preliminary hearing on Monday."

"Yes, Ted already contacted her. Margaret will testify on my behalf."

Elliot excused himself and left to take a shower. He let the warm water run over his body and tried to put his mind in order. *After the first night, I should have stopped seeing her.* He had returned home from that evening, glad that Ruth was in the Catskills, vowing to stop seeing Lindsey...but he continued their affair.

Lindsey's death haunted him. He didn't have the courage to think about their past together. He had known her intimately for five months. One night when she was feeling vulnerable she told Elliot about her life. Her father had left the family when she was thirteen. After married a younger woman, she lost touch with him. Lindsey was scarred by that traumatic event. She loved her father very much. Determined not to have to repeat the same fate, she vowed never to get married. She knew the divorce and remarriage had molded her character. She learned to be independent and to take care of herself.

Elliot felt drawn to her carefree spirit. On one of her journeys to the Far East she had joined a school that taught the art of love-making. One night she asked Elliot if he would like to be more adventurous and opened a drawer above her bed. Elliot couldn't believe his eyes. It was full of love-making apparatuses. She explained the purpose and use of each one. There was all kind of things to increase Lindsey's pleasure: vibrators in all kinds of shapes, textures and purpose. Also masks, clips, colorful robes and lingerie. There were items to be used to increase her partner's pleasure: feathers, metal beads on a chain, razors and long false nails.

Lindsey opened a small wooden ornate cabinet filled with different fragrances and oils, bottled in containers of different sizes and shapes. Each oil had its own unique property. She pointed out a few and explained their origin of the qualities they possessed.

Elliot had a good sexual relationship with Ruth but he had never ventured into territory beyond conventional love-making. With Lindsey it was an exploration into new experiences. At times, Lindsey initiated slow, passionate and sensual love. On other nights she would become wild and use one or more of her sex toys. At first, Elliot was reluctant to participate in these new adventures, but after a few times he grew to enjoy them.

On one occasion she said it would be her night to dominate him. Eliot was not allowed to move or touch her. They started with a Japanese bath, than Lindsey washed him thoroughly. Afterward in bed she massaged him with strong-smelling sensual oils. She rubbed them all over his body, which created a warm and exhilarating sensation. After that, she slowly and skillfully placed ice cubes on his body; the extreme sensations of warm and cool on his skin added extra stimulation. Elliot wanted to respond but was reminded not to move. This constraint enhanced his desire. She inserted a Japanese strand of silver beads connected by silk thread into his anus, pleasuring him to climatic ecstasy. A few times, just as he almost exploded, she stopped. Then, slowly, she began again until Elliot pleaded that he couldn't take it any longer. Lindsey let Elliot release himself, pulling the beads out at the same time, bringing Elliot sensations of joy that reached every cell of his body. She then allowed him to kiss her thankfully all over her body. She released her build-up at once, sharing his climax and her own.

11

The first meeting of the preliminary hearing convened on the Monday following Thanksgiving. Everything in the hearing room gave the surrealistic appearance of a theater stage, though the atmosphere was oddly upbeat as though some positive intention was being served.

"All rise," the court clerk announced. Judge Freemont appeared from the back door and took his seat. "Good morning," he said smiling.

Clarence Freemont, a fifty-two-year old African-American, was the presiding judge. A heavy-set man, he sat in his large leather chair like a king on a throne. The court reporter, a middle-aged woman with stiff hair and a clown-like dress of red and white polka dots, had her face glued to her stenograph. George flipped through his paperwork, acting as if ambivalent to the surroundings. Ted was giving Elliot last minute instructions. Ruth sat tensely in the back row, trying to control her emotions with deep breathing.

"We are on the record in the case of People vs. Barrett," Judge Freemont started the proceedings. "The defendant is present with counsel. The people are represented. The Deputy District Attorney may proceed."

"Thank you very much, Your Honor," George said.

George divided his case into three main aims. Firstly, to establish that there was an affair between Lindsey and Elliot; secondly to establish the connection of Elliot to the murder scene through fingerprints, hair samples and telephone calls between Lindsey and Elliot; thirdly, to establish a probable motive.

For his first witness, George put on the stand a thirty-two-year-old waitress named Patricia Gonzales who identified Elliot as being in the company of Lindsey on two separate occasions. He asked her the usual identifying questions: her name, location of the restaurant, and the exact time she had observed the couple.

"Can you please identify for the court the person you saw at the restaurant with the deceased, Ms. Lindsey Anderson?" George asked.

She pointed to Elliot. George had instructed her to speak up so her statement could be recorded.

"That man, the one sitting to the left of the lawyer," Patricia said shyly.

"On the two occasions you witnessed, were both of them friendly towards each other?"

"Objection!" Ted insisted loudly. "He is leading the witness."

"Sustained." Judge Freemont said.

"How would you say they behaved?" George asked.

"They were very friendly."

"What do you mean by 'very friendly'?"

"They were laughing, talking and showing interest in each other."

"Would you say they looked like lovers?"

"Objection. He's putting words in her mouth."

"Just state your objection," Judge Freemont declared. Ted nodded.

"How did they express their fondness for each other?" George asked.

"Like I said. Laughing, looking into each other's eyes, things like that."

"How long were they there?"

"About an hour and a half each time."

George pointed to a receipt in his hand. "Exhibit number twenty-two. May I approach the witness?" He did not wait for a response and handed Patricia the article.

"Are these your initials at the top of this credit card receipt?"

"Yes sir."

"Who paid the bill at the end of the dinner?"

"She did," Patricia said.

"You mean Ms. Lindsey?"

"Yes sir."

George asked a few more questions and then gave the floor to Ted for the cross examination.

Ted, with a soft charming voice, asked Patricia the usual introductory questions and then in a more authoritarian tone asked: "How long have you been working in this restaurant?"

"About nine months," Patricia replied quietly.

"What is the average number of customers you serve in a week?"

Patricia thought for a moment. "I can't say for sure."

"I'm not asking for an exact amount, just a rough estimation."

"Then I'll say a few hundred," she answered with hesitation.

"OK, a few hundred a week. Fair enough. How could you identify any specific customer who you have seen only twice and is not a regular, out of the thousand customers you have seen in the course of your employment?"

George looked intent. Patricia looked at him and then to the judge, a little confused. "I'm not comfortable answering that question…"

Ted felt elated whenever he could corner a witness, but had an immediate setback when she continued after an insistent instruction from the judge.

"Well… I am embarrassed… to say that Dr. Barrett got my attention because he is a handsome man who I felt attracted to."

Judge Freemont scornfully hushed giggles that erupted in the courtroom. Ted realized he had put himself into a trap, but knew how to recuperate fast.

"OK. You said they were very friendly. Were they holding hands? Were they seated on the same side of the table or opposing sides?"

"They sat opposite each other."

"Were they kissing?"

"No sir."

"So, you say they were simply friendly but not romantic?"

"Well, a little more than just friendly," Patricia insisted.

"Okay, a little bit," Ted agreed with a conciliating voice. "Did you hear any of their conversation?"

"No sir."

"So then it's just your opinion, not actual fact that you can state for certain."

"That's correct, sir. That is what I felt about what I observed." That's all Ted wanted to establish. "No more questions."

The next witness was Arnold Blumenthal, the owner of a gallery next to Lindsey's.

He testified he saw a Mercedes sedan, the same model, color and year of Elliot's car, parked in front of Lindsey's apartment at approximately 10:00 PM on the night of the murder. Ted argued that many Mercedes sedans were parked all over the city.

Ted knew that Elliot's car was dark blue and might be mistaken for black. He knew he could score with that witness but chose not to argue about it now.

George moved to his next line of questioning to tie Elliot to the crime scene. Paul McDavid was the first officer who arrived at the scene. He testified that Margaret came to Lindsey's apartment and found Lindsey's body on the couch two days after the murder. He secured the site and made initial investigations until the assigned detectives arrived one hour and forty minutes later.

George placed two photographs of Lindsey on the wall. One showed her smiling, full of vitality, with her hair blowing in the wind. The other showed her lying dead on the couch.

The clerk called Chief Homicide Detective Sills to the witness stand. He was an experienced officer who, having served thirty-five years on the force, had a relaxed manner on the witness stand. His gray suit added to his grandfatherly appearance, and his quiet, deep voice gave an impression of confidence and reliability.

Elliot felt the same repulsion toward Sills as he had in the interrogation room and on the day Sills had searched his home. He realized how very cleverly this detective had laid the trap into which he'd almost fallen. A few days after Ted bailed out Elliot he was called in again for questioning at the police station. This time Ted was present and followed every question very carefully.

After Detective Sills was sworn in, he answered George's adept questions, stating his description of the crime scene and his observations. "There was an apparent struggle," Detective Sills said, pointing to the enlarged photograph of Lindsey's dead body and the rows of diagrams. "These dark blue marks on both sides of her wrists were made by someone holding her forcefully." He theorized that the victim tried to relieve the grip and was shoved back forcefully, hit the chair, and then bumped the back of her head on the wooden side of the couch. He theorized that the killer then took the couch pillow and, still holding her hands above her head, suffocated her until she died.

George was pleased with the testimony. Ruth looked at Lindsey's beautiful portrait and then at the photograph of her dead body. How horrifying. She thought of the waste of such a promising life, and the sadness and pain that her mother had to endure. Elliot sat shocked, as if in a dream throughout the proceedings. He could not make himself look at the photographs. He could barely follow George's tedious questioning and the detailed answers from Sills.

The sight of the photographs bothered Ted, but he pushed it to the back of his mind. He sat tense in his seat, following every word, objecting to the slight irregularities and taking or receiving notes from his assistants. Ted listened to Sills' testimony, and thought how his distrust of police investigations was correct. They created a theory out of impressions derived from the crime scene. Some were correct and others were total speculation. Ted knew that Lindsey had struggled to free herself, but she was not pushed, and her hands were not held above her head. He did not suffocate her with a pillow.

He was disturbed by another fact that had escaped his attention. The photograph showed Lindsey with her face looking up at the ceiling, but his best recollection was that her face was left facing downward. He made a note to ask Margaret if she had touched the body or moved Lindsey's face to see if she were alive before calling the police. It was the first time he could hear the evidence as a lawyer and be able to personally dispute it. Yet he could not reveal the facts he knew beyond doubt.

George wrapped up the session with a final question. "So, your conclusion is that a killer murdered Lindsey on the night of the twenty-eighth of October?"

"Yes sir. I'm certain without a doubt it was a murder."

12

Standing together in the courthouse hallway, Ted, Elliot, and Ruth summed up the events of the first day in court. The effects of this long day showed on their weary faces. "How do you think it went?" Ruth asked Ted.

"I told you and Elliot before," Ted said, "it's like a see-saw. One minute you're up and the next you're down. Today went fine. They were well prepared and so were we."

"Should we expect any surprises?" Ruth asked.

"No surprises. It doesn't work like in the movies. I already know through discovery everything they know."

Elliot's seemed agonized and Ted tempered his words. "Elliot, I noticed you were a bit spacey in the courtroom. The judge observes everyone's reactions, especially yours. Remember what I said, you must look relaxed and confident. Tomorrow is another important day. Let's go home to gather our strength."

"I hate to sit there all day. I would prefer to be with my patients back in the operating room."

"Hopefully, we will get you there soon, but it won't help if you're not focused."

Ruth nodded in agreement with Ted.

"I'll try to be aware of it tomorrow."

"Try is not good enough, Elliot. You must succeed. Now let's get a good night's sleep."

"Ted is right," Ruth said with concern. "It's not a pleasure for me to sit in the courtroom either, but we must do all we can."

The next morning at 9:30 everyone was present in the court-room. George spent the morning continuing his direct questioning of Detective Sills' testimony. He managed to prove that Elliot's fingerprints and hair samples were found in Lindsey's bathroom and on her living room couch. Telephone records established a direct link between Lindsey and Elliot.

Ted spent the afternoon in cross-examination, deciding to adopt his favorite tactic of attacking the credibility of the police. He pounded Sills with questions about his conclusions, but Sills was not trapped by Ted's provocative line of questioning. He maintained his relaxed manner and answered questions with a constant slight smile.

"Would you be able to testify for certain when Dr. Barrett's fingerprints were made in Lindsey's apartment?"

"No. All I can tell you are the locations where they were found." He paused for a second and, with more emphasis he added, "And that the fingerprints certainly belong to Elliot."

"O.K., what if they were placed there a few days earlier than the crime date?"

"Like I said before, we can only say that his fingerprints were found in the apartment, and where they were found."

To Ted's questions about the hair samples, the answer was the same. Sills admitted that he could not place any witness who saw Elliot that day around the crime scene. Ted also managed to obtain an answer that the content of the telephone conversation was unknown.

At the end of another tiresome day, Ruth and Elliot felt that Ted had managed to place doubt on the theory George trying to establish. Ted complimented Elliot on his improved demeanor in the courtroom and warned them both not to draw any conclusions about the outcome.

Over the next days, George questioned his next witness, the chief coroner. Dr. Khallil Rajestan. He had dark skin, piercing black eyes, and wore a white cotton Sikh head covering. Dr. Rajestan sat erect with his head up, listening attentively to the judge's instructions.

"Can you state your duty for the court?" George asked.

"I am a forensic pathologist who performs autopsies to determine the cause and manner of death on the deceased that come under our jurisdiction." He spoke with a heavy Indian accent. His testimony estimated the time of death at between 9:45 P.M. and 12:00 P.M. The contents of her digestive system consisted of wine and Thai food. No drugs were found. Dr. Rajestan explained the marks of struggle on her body. He concluded the cause of death to be a strong blow to the back of the head, and the use of the couch pillow to suffocate Lindsey.

Ted questioned the precision of the time of death but the coroner insisted on the correctness of his answer. Ted could not reveal how he knew otherwise, and had to retreat from further inquiry. He challenged Dr. Rajestan's theory that Lindsey was suffocated with a pillow. The day before Ted had asked Margaret about the position of Lindsey's head. She told him she had turned Lindsey's head when she first found her, but was almost certain she placed the head back to its initial position.

Ted decided to risk further inquiry on the subject of sour suffocation. "What if, after the blow to the head, the body ended up facing the couch? Can it be that the suffocating occurred that way?"

"The body was found with her head facing away from the couch. Therefore that could not have happened," the coroner insisted.

"The question is theoretical. If we assume that the police or Margaret actually found her head facing down, would that be a possibility?" Ted asked.

"Objection!" George shouted, not understanding this line of questioning.

Judge Freemont asked the attorneys to approach the bench. Ted explained that there might be a possibility that Lindsey's head was facing downward when Margaret found her. He was only asking a theoretical question. Judge Freemont agreed, but insisted that it needed to be clear that the question was theoretical.

"Can you answer the question?" Ted continued after the judge issued his stipulation.

"If she was alive right after the blow to the head, and lost consciousness, and then fell directly on the pillow without the ability to breathe... it might be a possibility…but in my estimation, it's a slim one." Ted himself was confused about the issue but did not want to press it further for fear he would blunder.

"Was there any evidence found under Lindsey's fingernails?"

"No sir."

This time it was Ted who managed to have the final word of the day. George felt his witness had held up well under Ted's pressure and was hoping to complete his direct questioning the next day. He believed he managed to convey his objectives clearly enough to win the case and go to trial.

Ted drove to his house, still haunted by the coroner's testimony, and the photographs taken of Lindsey's after she died. *Did I leave Lindsey still alive; face down to be suffocated by the pillow, after I left? Did she wake up drunk on the couch and suffocate herself?* She had had a few glasses of wine. The time of death that Dr. Rajestan had established also troubled him. Did Lindsey die later that night? Had he been in too much of a panic to double-check to see if she were really dead? *Detective Sills didn't thoroughly investigate the source of the food contents. If he had, he could possibly trace it to me. Did anyone notice the Jaguar parked in the alley?* By assuming Elliot was the suspect, George had neglected to consider some important evidence.

Heather was at the door when he arrived home, wearing a sexy nightgown. Lights were dimmed and dinner was on the table. Ted was not in the mood to discuss the case, but didn't want to hurt Heather's feelings. He kissed her and then went to take a shower to relax and wash away the strains of the day. The immensity of it all was difficult for him to bear.

They sat at the table and ate silently; Heather respected his withdrawal, knowing how to read him when he was under stress. After dinner, Ted asked to be forgiven. "Heather, I'm sorry about tonight. I know you went to a lot of trouble to try to create a special mood. It was a big day and I have a lot on my mind. I need to go to sleep early."

"It's all right. I'm fine." She gave him a hug and led him to the bedroom. She helped him take off his clothes and covered him with a blanket. "Good night, my love. Sleep well," she whispered lovingly.

Heather's concern touched Ted. The first time he met Heather, she was a flight attendant on a flight he was on to visit his mother. Heather asked if he wanted a drink. She had a bright smile and an innocent glow. During the flight they struck up a conversation, and he managed to charm her into giving him her telephone number.

Six months earlier he had finished a nasty divorce and went on wild sprees with women as if he were back in college. Ted remembered how Elliot had tried to talk some sense into him about his wild lifestyle. Ted liked to tell Elliot about the pleasure of hunting and conquering the many women he seduced. He proudly bragged to Elliot that he had a robust libido, and that his lack of inhibitions was more truthful than appearing to have a repressed monogamous sex life. Elliot responded by insisting he was not repressed, and his sex life was deeply satisfying in a way Ted could not understand. Elliot told Ted he was trying to recapture his youth by going out with younger women and suggested that the sense of novelty found in his conquests could be found in other ways. He even mentioned a study that showed that the hormonal effect of the first encounter between lovers is intoxicating but fades away as the relationship stabilized. He suggested that Ted enter therapy to discover why he had a fear of intimacy.

At the age of forty, Ted was ready to settle down again. In a few weeks he convinced Heather to move in with him. At first, it was great. Heather was away flying and Ted could secretly continue his lifestyle. Later Ted asked her to stop working, so she could attend more to his needs. Heather thought that twenty-six was a good age to have children and stay home. She found herself attending to Ted's every need and neglecting her own. Soon, she found him coming home with lipstick on his shirt collar. Other telltale signs proved to her that he was having affairs. She started to focus on her physical appearance, spent hours at the gym and became consumed with trying out exotic diets. She even had breast implants, thinking the improvement would make her more attractive to him. Ted had been attracted to Heather's vigorous young spirit. He saw her change into a self-conscious person who was losing her individual will. Without either of them noticing, their relationship plunged into resentment and jealousy, and they lost the little they had in common. When he met Lindsey, seven years later, Ted was ready to divorce Heather.

Now Ted was beginning to realize how much Heather really loved him, and how much he was to blame for their drifting apart. Tonight he realized that he valued Heather's concern, and thought he might regain an appreciation of her simple but loving qualities. He even thought to surprise her in the morning with his suggestion to start a series of fertility treatments so they might have children. With that comforting thought, he turned toward Heather, embracing her warmth, and fell asleep.

Dressing in the morning, Ted realized that Elliot's relationship with Lindsey continued to plague him. *How ironic that Elliot had to meet Lindsey to introduce him to the temptations he was preaching against. Apparently Elliot was after this hormone effect also. How odd that we both ended up enjoying the same woman. Elliot had fallen under her spell.* He couldn't picture how shy, conservative Elliot and wild, free Lindsey could find anything in common. Or maybe Elliot was encountering his own dark side and couldn't admit it, even to himself. Ted thought that their relationship was close enough for Elliot to feel comfortable enough to confide in him about his affair. *It's funny to think of Elliot being ashamed.*

13

"The people rest," George announced after he finished interrogating his last witness.

"Do you have any motions at this time to be heard with regard to any motion?" Judge Freemont asked Ted.

"Yes, Your Honor. At this point we would like to make a motion to have this case dismissed."

"That motion is denied."

"Your Honor, we will like to be heard on a motion to dismiss," Ted said.

"I'll hear you at this time."

"Thank you," Ted said and started his argument. "This is a case based entirely on circumstantial evidence. Through our cross-examination and the people's presentation, it can be either a theory toward suspicion of guilt or of innocence." Ted continued his argument that what the people consider as physical evidence could be explained easily by Elliot's admittance of visiting the apartment on occasions before to the murder date. Since the investigator was unable to fix the age of the physical evidence, it is equally reasonable to assume that it was placed there much earlier.

"This is clearly a case in which everyone has jumped to immediate conclusions regarding the evidence presented. I feel strongly that this case is not ready to come to court. At this point, I do not see any basis for any strong suspicion that Dr. Barrett is guilty of anything," Ted said, looking directly at Judge Freemont. "Therefore, Your Honor, it's incumbent upon you under the law to exercise your duty and dismiss this case."

"Mr. Goodman, please state your argument," Judge Freemont said.

"Thank you, Your Honor," George said. "We cannot ignore all the consistent and strong physical evidence, the defendant's fingerprints and hair sample. There are many telephone conversations between him and the deceased, obviously more than necessary to communicate with a patient's daughter. We also have a witness who connected the defendant to the crime and directly to the victim. We have a witness who saw the accuser's car the night of the crime and a waitress who saw the defendant with the deceased. All of these facts clearly tie Dr. Barrett to the crime. There is cause to show that the defendant indeed committed the crime he is charged with." George continued his argument, point by point, showing Elliot's connection to Lindsey and to the crime scene. "We also request at this point that the defendant to be placed under custody of the sheriff."

After George finished his summation Judge Freemont called for a lunch recess. Outside the courtroom Elliot and Ruth, visibly stressed, told Ted they were impressed with his presentation and felt the Judge would dismiss the case. Ted thought they were whistling in the dark.

When they returned from the lunch recess, the judge was ready to rule. "The court has carefully considered the argument of counsel and the evidence in this case. The court feels that there is ample evidence to establish strong suspicions of guilt for the accused. Therefore, the motion to dismiss is denied."

Elliot was stunned when the Judge asked him to stand and proceeded to tell him that it appeared from the evidence presented that the following offenses had been committed by him. He listed all the counts of alleged guilt and the reference to all violations of the Penal Code. He allowed the extension of the bail with no need for custody of the sheriff at this point.

Ted never liked to lose a court case. The judge had ruled that there was enough evidence to tie Elliot to the crime and ruled a trial would take place at a later date. It was not so much of a strain for

Ted as the pang of guilt he felt for being responsible for Lindsey's death. Not giving his best efforts on Elliot's behalf in the preliminary hearing made him feel worse. Ted realized that Elliot would stick to his declaration of innocence. He would never agree to plea bargain. Ted feared that in losing the case, he might be sending his friend to many years of incarceration.

Everything is getting too far out of hand. It must stop, Ted thought. *Elliot has suffered enough. I wanted some suffering but … After all, I'm responsible for Lindsey's death. I always did my best trying a case. I must work much harder now than I had ever worked before to free Elliot.*

Ted could barely handle Elliot's and Ruth's disappointments. "We thought that the preliminary hearing would end this nightmare," Ruth stammered with a tear-stained face.

"You said you could prevent a trial." Elliot sighed, broken in spirit. "I need to get back to work."

"What about the trial?" Ruth asked, immediately thinking in practical terms.

"That's a completely different ball game," Ted said with conviction. "The trial jury is a completely independent body. We'll hire an expert to study the jurors and we'll have much more input, such as which witnesses we would or would not like as members of the jury."

"What will be different about the evidence they present?" Elliot asked.

"We have much more leeway. I have a few surprises in mind."

"What kind of surprises? I thought you said no new surprises would be allowed," Ruth probed.

"I thought about a few things that did not come up in the preliminary hearing," Ted said. "I'm planning to introduce a few points to shed light on new evidence that would raise doubts necessary to bring about Elliot's acquittal. Listen guys, I'm exhausted. Let's get together for dinner tomorrow and we can discuss my tactics."

On their way home Ruth asked Elliot if they should consider his father's suggestion to bring in more help for Ted's defense team. "The trial is much more complicated than the preliminary hearing," she said. "Your father knows quite a few good lawyers in Boston…"

"I do not want to hear anything more about this…" Elliot muttered.

"But…"

"No buts about it," Elliot said annoyed. "I have all my faith in Ted. He is my friend and he is doing a good job." Ruth realized there was nothing else that she could say. *He found a really good time to prove his independence from his parents*, she thought sarcastically. *We need all the help we can get right now.* They drove in silence all the way home.

Elliot went to sleep early, but Ruth remained awake, full of worries. Recent events had forced her to rethink her life, particularly the past month. Elliot seemed to be drawing more into himself. The man that had always been so strong was no longer there. She could not lean on him emotionally and she needed to go inside herself to find the strength she needed to deal with issues she had never had to face. She hated to deal with the telephone calls, the endless explanations of what had happened and how she and Elliot were handling the situation. She now had duties at Elliot's office, to take care of the administration, to help refer his patients to other doctors and to solve other problems. She kept up communication with their worried children. And she had to keep cope with Elliot's ongoing depression.

The next morning she got a call from Texas. It was Debbie, her sister. "Sis, my darling, I was so sorry to hear the news about Elliot. This just cannot be. I know Elliot is not capable of such things. What are you going to do?"

"Elliot, of all people. Can you believe it? We are still in shock," Ruth said sadly, "We are assessing the situation and choosing the next course of action."

"How is Elliot taking all of this?"

"Not so well," Ruth said. "Actually he is taking it hard. To be wrongfully accused is hard for anybody to take."

"Is there anything I can do?"

"You really are a sweetheart, but what can be done?" Ruth asked.

"Listen, I can take some time off and come to be with you all."

"I love you Debbie, and I appreciate your concern. This call has made my day. Actually you *can* do something for me. Please talk to the rest of the family and calm them down. Everything here will be all right."

"The whole family loves you and prays everything will end up fine."

"Thanks, we need all the help we can get," Ruth said, encouraged. Ruth thought of her family in Texas, and how she had never again expected to feel that sense of security she'd had back home.

The next day George met Ted at the courthouse. "One point for me and one for you," George said with humor.

"Punching below the belt, huh?" Ted said, pretending to be insulted. "Let's see how you score in the trial."

"Seriously Ted, I thought you had more juice in you than what you gave in the court." George laughed, and immediately realized he said something that affected and hurt Ted. "I was just kidding, of course," he said to Ted, but he'd actually expressed what he really thought of Ted's performance. Choppy work at best, some downright confusing. He knew Ted would be much sharper in the courtroom.

"I reserve my energy for the real trial," Ted said, pretending he was on top of the situation.

"We need to get together to set schedules for the trial." George said. George was careful not to yield to the City Hall pressure to quickly try murder cases. He had developed an instinct for reading people. He observed their body language, postures and facial muscles; rubbing their eyes when trying to cover a lie. These signs revealed conscious and unconscious intentions they tried to hide. He knew for certain Ted was not at his best. Elliot's behavior in the courtroom confirmed George's conviction to bring him to trial. He was definitely hiding something. He knew Elliot's relaxed manner was a result of coaching, not of innocence.

Ted left the courthouse to go to his office. With a serious tone and raised eyebrows Melissa announced, "It's Mr. Barrett on the line."

"Elliot…" Ted spoke to the phone.

"It's Elliot's father, Mr. Barrett speaking."

"Mr. Barrett. How are you?"

"Could be better."

"How can I help you?"

"I just received the news. Listen Ted, can I speak to you truthfully?"

"I cannot discuss Elliot's case with anyone."

"Oh no, I understand. What I wanted to say is that Elliot did not want my lawyer to help you. I respect that, although I wish he did. I would like to say that I will go to any means necessary to set Elliot free. You know money is not an issue. That will be between us, of course."

"Thank you, but it will not be necessary."

"Are you going to have anyone else with you…? I mean to help you?"

"I am planning to create a special team that will dedicate their time solely to this case. We already spoke to an expert that will help in the jury selection."

"That's good, that's good. I'm placing Elliot in your hands."

"You should rest assured that we will do everything, and I mean everything, to set him free."

"Thank you Ted. Come visit us when all this is over."

Ted hung up the phone feeling agitated. *Elliot's father is really out of line.* He appreciated Elliot's full confidence in him and his rejection of his father's interference. He realized he had not even discussed lawyer's fees with Elliot, but he was definitely not going to accept payment from his father. At this time he didn't want to decide how to handle payment from Elliot. The hours and resources needed for a thorough trial would cost hundreds of thousands of dollars. *Elliot would not have any trouble paying that amount, but how can you charge to defend a crime of which you, yourself, are guilty?*

Ted pushed that thought to the back of his mind.

Eating breakfast on the morning after the decision to go to trial, Ruth felt the silence in the room and the distance between her and Elliot. She was disturbed with the loss and disturbed by what she heard in the testimony. "I feel you are not being straight with me, Elliot. You told me there was nothing at all between you and Lindsey."

Elliot felt panic. In the past weeks Elliot thought he would come clean, tell Ruth that he had a short affair with Lindsey. It tormented him having to lie over and over again. But he was afraid to face Ruth, who had been so loving and trusting during this trying time. What kind of excuse could he come up with to explain his behavior?

Elliot decided to stick to his lies. "I meant nothing romantically. Why are you asking?"

"Why in God's name were you in her apartment so many times?"

"Not so many times. Only a few." Seeing Ruth's raised eyebrows he added, "She told me she had a rare art collection and I figured I'd come to visit her mother and also see the collection. It was a really an interesting collection."

"OK, let's say that is plausible. What did you do with her in the restaurant?"

Elliot felt he was too far invested in his deceit to back down now. "Lindsey was a very interesting woman. She had intellectual gifts. She knew about art and the philosophy of the Far East. I didn't think it was out of line… what was so wrong to sit there and learn from Lindsey"

"So why all this secrecy? Couldn't you tell me about her? You could have invited her here to our home so I could learn too."

"You're right. I didn't think about it. I confused it in my mind as part of the attention I gave Margaret."

"I never want to mention it again after today," Ruth said, unconvinced. "But please, Elliot. I need to know if there is anything else you are hiding from me. To go through all this hell and humiliation... I need to trust you totally."

Elliot could not control his emotions any longer, and said with teary eyes. "Ruth, you must believe me. I love you."

Ruth hugged Elliot and laid her head on his chest. "I believe you. The issue is closed."

14

Ted was heading to the courthouse to meet George and receive a trial date and learn who was going to be the assigned judge. Traffic was impossibly slow during the winter months. The mud and slush that followed the few days of snow got everything dirty, spoiling his mood even more. The endless flow of pedestrians who filled the sidewalks always bothered him. Shop windows were screaming with ads for all kinds of sales. The streets seemed like a river of people moving in unison to a definite destination—shopping. He didn't understand the fuss made about Christmas. He viewed it as a mass hysteria of people who felt compelled to shop every year. He thought that all the American holidays were basically an excuse for selling merchandise.

As a goodwill gesture toward Heather, this Christmas Ted agreed to share Christmas dinner with her family in New Jersey. He asked her to spare his agony and do the pleasant shopping for him. Heather was happy to comply. She enjoyed the recent shift in their relationship. Ted was busy with Elliot's case, but now he would call her from work just to see how she was doing. He made an effort to eat dinner at home and spent more time with Heather. He expressed a more attentive attitude toward her during lovemaking, a bit violent and exciting, and with an almost desperate clinging that Heather enjoyed.

Ted arrived at the courthouse, ran up the stairs, and met George in the hallway. "We got Judge Meredith Boyd," George said, disappointed.

"Cranky Granny," Ted replied with a chuckle.

"Yeah, she's a tough old cookie." Both laughed.

They entered her office as she impatiently waved them in. Her large office was covered with bookshelves from floor to ceiling. The room was dark, and her desk was opposite the entry door, which forced everyone who entered to walk across the large space where the judge could observe them. Her skinny body almost disappeared as she seated herself in a large chair. She was in her mid-sixties, with a long face and small eyes that seemed like they had never smiled.

"Please sit down," she said. Without waiting, continued. "I want to set the trial date for Monday, the twelfth of January."

"That's a good date for us," George said.

"I would like a little bit more time to prepare," Ted said.

"That should give you enough time. I want to get on with it," she said in a definitive tone.

"There is Christmas, then the New Year…" Ted tried to argue.

"We can start jury selection whenever you are ready." She ignored Ted's comment. Ted knew better than to get on the bad side of a judge even before the trial started.

George said that the District Attorney would like to agree to have the proceedings be televised. "We are not a circus," she said. "There will be no television in my courtroom." The issue was closed. She gave them the rest of the instructions as to how she liked to run her courtroom, and what she expected from them. Her stern mannerisms created a distance that was hard to bridge. She would not respond at all to Ted's charming humor and showed her discouragement as if it were a nuisance. "We are going to get together right away with the pretrial preparations, I want everything to move swiftly and efficiently." George gave a quick glance at Ted, and his ironic smile did not escape Judge Boyd's attention. She elected not to react.

In the following weeks, they met in her chamber to go through the pretrial Proceedings, the technical issues that arose concerned with various legal matters. At the same time, jury selection started. The tedious process of jury selection was the aspect of law that Ted disliked most. Thousands of people had to disrupt their lives to perform their civic duty. The court administration divided them into groups to be sent to their assigned courts. Ted and George would receive hundreds of potential jurors for instructions and interviews, until they finally agreed on twelve jurors plus two alternates. Judge Boyd ruled against sequestering the jury.

Ted did not spare any amount of money necessary for experts to analyze each prospective juror. They designed a well-planned questionnaire created specifically for this case. The goal was to select jurors who had respect for people with money and position, who believed that police could not be trusted and who could be manipulated into being doubtful—people who would view Lindsey's lifestyle as wrong—preferably, a majority of conservative middle-class women, including African-Americans.

"This is the place where money talks," Ted explained to Elliot and Ruth. "We clearly have the advantage. We have the right to reject up to twelve jurors just because we do not like them. From our questioning we know them inside and out. People who do not have the financial resources we have don't have the same chance in the system."

"That is sad," Ruth said.

"That's what we have to work with. It's important that a few people like you can set Elliot free, whereas people that don't …" Ted realized his mistake of implicating Elliot, and corrected himself. "It's better that a few criminals slip through the cracks, than innocent people like you go to jail."

"That's right," Ruth exclaimed. "How could the system take a person like Elliot thus far? Where is the justice?"

"Justice will be at the end of the trial when we win," Ted said with forced conviction.

"I've heard that many innocent people are in jail. There was a profile on television of an attorney—I don't remember his name—who dedicated his life to freeing those victims. He spoke of thousand cases of innocent people in jail."

"This is probably the best system in the world," Ted said, uneasy with the conversation. Here he was an instrument causing undue harm to Elliot. "Be assured it's not going to be the case with Elliot. We have all the means to make this a certainty."

Elliot took advantage of time before the trial to plunge into his work. His office and clinic were located in Hospital Row on the East Side. The concentration of research and healthcare facilities, between York Avenue and FDR Drive, offered a spectacular view of the Queensboro Bridge. In summer, the gardens were a pleasant place to take a lunch break and watch the water. Now in winter the grounds were bare. Paths were barely visible beneath the snow.

Elliot was part of a faculty that had earned a worldwide reputation. He was part of the most prestigious research facility in the nation that counted among its renowned patients the former Shah of Iran. Elliot liked his daily routine of making rounds and seeing patients. Mostly, he loved the operating room. He enjoyed psyching himself up during the tedious ritual of hand washing. He loved the use of his expertise and the concentration needed to perform surgery. He was known as a perfectionist who liked to manage the tiniest detail of the whole process.

Ruth quit her job and continued to help Elliot organize work left neglected. They decided that the best course of action was to get back to their normal life routine, as much as possible. Christmas was a few days away, and Ruth tried to overcome her distractions and enjoy a little holiday spirit. Talking to Ted, she felt optimistic about the outcome of the trial. She decided not to change her traditional way of shopping for gifts. She asked Elliot to join her. He rejected the idea.

Ruth took the afternoon off and taxied to Fifth Avenue, where she enjoyed the window displays. She loved Manhattan at this time of the year. The exhilarating atmosphere helped her to forget her troubles, and she joined in Manhattan's Christmas spirit. People seemed different around this time of the year. Even the cold weather did not dampen their spirits. The dazzling tree decorations and the dramatically designed shop windows attracted millions of tourists who became infatuated with the city.

Ruth enjoyed walking among the people. There were faces, clothing and languages from many nationalities flowing together in the same human stream. In front of the New York Public Library at 42nd street, a circle of people sang Christmas carols. In front of St. Patrick's Cathedral on 50th Street a uniformed soldier of the Salvation Army smiled and thanked her for her generous donation. She walked up the stairs and entered the church. She enjoyed the impressive Gothic architecture and the ornamental design of Lady Chapel behind the altar. Feeling the silence that the enormous space created, she felt compelled to pray. Ruth closed her eyes and silently, with deep longing, asked that her life return to normal. She opened her eyes and saw the image of Mary staring at her beyond the altar. Transfixed by the image of her peaceful face, she felt strength and hope.

Back outside, she turned into the crowded avenue, decorated with white winged angels leading to Rockefeller Plaza. A city-within-a-city, the vast subterranean promenade connected buildings, shops and restaurants. The Plaza's huge famous Christmas tree stood in front of the packed skating rink, enclosed by the tall art deco buildings.

She loved buying presents and seeing the happiness in her family's faces as they opened them. Her shopping started at Saks. She went through her long list and made large purchases to be wrapped at the store before delivery to her home. She continued walking North on upper Fifth Avenue all the way to Henri Bendel's. It's lavish quarters were connected by winding staircases sweeping up through its many stories. There she purchased gifts for her family and friends most close to her heart. She felt happy and full of accomplishment during the taxi ride taking her back home.

Every year, Ruth, Elliot and their children flew to Texas to celebrate Christmas. Debbie called to make sure this year would not be an exception. Elliot tried to resist the idea, but Ruth insisted.

"It will do us good to get out of New York, to breathe the open air at my parents' ranch," she said. "You've been given approval to leave the state. Ted said it would be fine."

"You didn't object when we didn't go to my parents' for Thanksgiving."

"Please, Elliot. I need a break from all this pressure. You can do this for me. Caroline and Jonathan want to go too." Elliot knew Ruth was under pressure. He knew that he had not been easy to live with the past few months and decided to concede. It proved to be a good idea. From the first moment they landed at the Dallas-Fort Worth airport, they felt the warmth of Ruth's family. Ruth's parents and all her sisters waited at the gate and shouted with glee, embracing each other with affection. Everyone was talking at once during the ride to the ranch.

The weather was more pleasant than the freezing cold of Manhattan, and the blue sky was a relief from New York City's gray weather. They drove down the five-lane highway to the range a few miles west of the city. The large log home was perfectly situated on a small hill surrounded by a meadow. Horses ran freely and, with wild gallops, accompanied the incoming cars. In the distance, longhorn cows grazed peacefully.

Ruth felt the heavy load of the recent events falling from her shoulders, replaced with the sense of comfort and security of her home, and the company of her loving family. Deep down she felt that Texas was still her home and Manhattan, a temporary residence. It was still hard for her to return to New York after each visit to her parents and siblings.

That afternoon Ruth and Debbie went for a ride with the horses. The children watched a Dallas Cowboys game with their cousins. Elliot rested on a hammock watching the sunset descend in a splendid array of golden hues. He tried to forget his worries, to enjoy the spectacular sunset and the soothing effects of the surrounding nature. He realized how far he was from his usual self, and how much the stress was draining energy from him.

On Christmas nights, Ruth's family gathered round a huge table. Ruth's father and some of her sisters' husbands stood around the large metal barrel that was converted to a charcoal barbecue. They were turning huge pieces of meat, while Ruth's mother and her daughters set the table. The children played together, enjoying each other's company. Elliot was amused by the informality of the event in contrast to how his family celebrated Christmas. Everyone here was dressed in casual clothing, the men in leather boots, blue jeans and belts with wide silver buckles and large cowboy hats. The women and the girls were dressed in similar style, some wearing full, bright skirts.

After dinner, everyone gathered around the fireplace in the spacious living room. A few musical instruments were brought out and everyone joined in singing Christmas songs. Elliot enjoyed the simple hospitality, and the union and love Ruth's family felt for one another. He was deeply touched, watching Ruth's glittering face and her happy interaction with her family.

The court case and its worries were pushed away. No one wanted to spoil the mood. Ruth's family would not ask questions unless Elliot volunteered information on his own. That night Elliot and Ruth made love passionately, savoring the momentary pleasure and intimacy of their rekindled passion.

15

For New Year's Eve, Ruth and Elliot were invited to Ted and Heather's apartment. Ted had a large penthouse on the corner of West 67th Street facing Central Park. The apartment was decorated in an ultra-modern Italian style, with a pale yellow leather couch and a peach-veined marble fireplace. Sculptures and a beautiful array of colorful Venetian glass and artifacts were on display. The walls were covered with paintings in various styles.

Ruth had never liked Ted's taste in clothing, or the way he decorated his apartment. She liked the rustic style and had learned to appreciate the classic architecture and taste favored by Elliot. *There is no sense of place; there is no harmony among the element,* Ruth thought, not realizing Ted had noticed her displeasure. "What a diverse collection, Ted," she said, diplomatically. "You bought some new pieces. I didn't know you were such an art lover."

"I love art, but mostly it was bought for investment value. Some of the pieces have gone up considerably in value since I bought them." Ted immediately realized he had made a mistake. Quite a few of the paintings has been purchased from Lindsey's gallery.

He turned abruptly, walking toward the kitchen to hide his red face. In a moment, he returned smiling, holding a gold tray and four tall crystal glasses. "Let's drink some champagne, wash it down with a shot of cold vodka and finish with excellent Russian caviar for the New Year," he announced festively. They each picked up a glass and stood around the fireplace, enjoying the warmth and appreciating the excellent champagne.

"Let's go to the dining room," Heather said. "Where there's

a great view of the skyline." Large windows in the dining room showed off the high-rise buildings surrounding Central Park. Beneath them glowed the spectacular lighting of the Tavern on the Green restaurant interwoven around the tree trunks and branches. Silver candleholders with tapers lit up the dining room, adding to the festive mood. The trays of the catered food were kept warm in silver chafing dishes. The serving chef took special care in presenting a variety of meat, fish, and vegetable dishes. The chef also recommended a good selection of wine poured into crystal glasses. "The table is arranged perfectly," Ruth complimented Heather, "and the food looks so special."

"We had it prepared by an old client of Ted's, a chef in a famous restaurant," Heather said. The food was great and they had a good time drinking wine and eating heartily. Heather and Ruth found a moment together in the kitchen while Ted and Elliot drank Remy Martin Cognac and smoked Havana cigars.

"Since Thanksgiving we've been doing great. Couldn't be better," Heather happily confided. "He even went with me to my family for Christmas Eve. How is Elliot doing?"

"I'm really happy for you. Elliot is preoccupied with the trial and, until it's over, I feel he won't find any peace."

"How are you doing?"

"Oh, I'm holding on. It's been real hard but I must be strong. Somebody must be, for the family's sake. This waiting time is adding to the apprehension, kind of driving us nuts."

"How are the children doing?"

"They stay in school and I try not to worry them. They should continue their lives as normally as possible. Let's join the guys. It's almost midnight," Ruth said.

"Ruth, anytime you need to talk, please feel free to come over or we can meet somewhere."

"Thanks, Heather."

"It's one minute to midnight; let's got out on the balcony," Ted yelled from the living room and opened the door to the balcony.

They drank champagne and stood outside in the cold but fresh, snowy air. At exactly midnight, the annual New Year's Run around Manhattan began. At the same time, a spectacular display of fireworks lit the sky, announcing the beginning of 1998. Runners filled the street, moving in waves like a mighty flowing river. From all the buildings, loud roars and whistles of cheering people filled the air.

"Yaaaahoooo, Happy New Year!" Ruth shouted with her Texan accent.

"Yaaaahoooo!" everyone yelled, imitating Ruth's accent and roaring with laughter. They exchanged hugs and kisses, blessing each other for a truly Happy New Year.

"What a spectacular sight," Heather said, gesturing to the waves of runners.

"Who in their right mind would run on such a freezing night?" Elliot asked.

"I think it's a great affirmation to start the New Year on such a positive note," Ruth said.

"Hey Elliot, do you want to pledge that when we win the trial we will promise to run together next year?" Ted challenged Elliot.

"Are you insane? Even if they released me from a hanging rope I wouldn't be that crazy." They all laughed as they toasted to the success of the trial and the evening wound to a close.

I can't believe I was such an idiot, Ted thought immediately after the Barrett's left his apartment. *There are so many things I bought from Lindsey. Could Elliot have spotted them? Could Ruth have put two and two together?*

"Heather, what did you talk to Ruth about in the kitchen?" He tried to sound nonchalant.

"Just women talk. I told her how much we are in love and she told me Elliot was real worried."

"That's all?"

"That's all. Why are you asking?"

"Oh nothing. Just asking. By the way—the whole evening was such a success thanks to you. You did a great job."

"Thanks honey. You kept the whole evening going."

"Let me show you one greater thing I can do for you tonight," he said carrying her into the bedroom.

"You know what happens when you drink too much," Heather teased, "Are you sure you can deliver?"

"Hey, you haven't seen nothin' yet," Ted bragged humorously.

"It will take you the whole night," she continued, teasingly. "But I love it," she said in a sexy voice.

Ted had a hard time getting aroused. Heather continued with her teasing game and started to provocatively rub her body against his. Heather's actions and the earlier art conversation brought Lindsey to mind. Ted started fantasizing about the time he had spent with Lindsey during one of her sex games. With renewed vitality, he entered Heather and engulfed himself in slow stroking movements, feeling Heather welcoming him inside.

Pictures ran through his mind in rapid memory flashes. He remembered the first time he went to the gallery. Lindsey sat at an antique desk and welcomed him with a smile. From the moment he laid eyes on her he felt a strong sexual chemistry that motivated him to pursue her. She wore tight black leather pants that clung to her tall legs, barely leaving to the imagination the content between her thighs. Her red silk blouse followed the curves of her breasts, exposing the contour of nipples beneath the thin material.

Ted expounded his intention to buy art for investment value as well as aesthetics.

In a businesslike and confident manner, Lindsey gave him an impressive presentation of her ability and knowledge. He followed her through the gallery, paying more attention to her body than her words. Ted started to visit the gallery regularly and bought many pieces. At first, she didn't show any interest beyond helping him with art purchases, but his aggressive manner appealed to her and over time and they began having intense sexual encounters.

He was immediately receptive to her sexual openness. They seemed to bring out each other's most extreme sexual tendencies.

Ted was proud that he was satisfying her sexual appetite. She taught him how to be patient until she was ready to receive her pleasure. A picture from one particular night surfaced in Ted's mind as he made love to his wife. Lindsey had told Ted that she wanted him to totally dominate her. "Everything goes," she said.

"Everything?" he asked, immediately interested.

"Let your imagination go."

He plunged into the game with vigor and passion. He demanded she dress as a prostitute and when she pretended to hesitate, he forcefully tore her clothes off. He pulled her to her dresser and chose provocative lingerie for her to wear. She obeyed, pretending she was frightened of his anger. She put on long, false eyelashes, dark eyeliner and red lipstick. Aroused by her transformation, he forced her on the bed and tied her hands and her legs to the bed. Using profanity, he forced himself on her, not bothering to take off her costume. She pretended to plead for his mercy, which stimulated him even more. He did not listen to her pleas until emitting a loud moan, he was satisfied.

Ted remembered how he had surprised her by leaving her tied to the bed. He dressed and said that it was getting late and he must get home. "I did not like this kind of game," he said with a grin. At first Lindsey thought it was part of the game, but when he did not return she was frightened. He pretended to walk down the staircase and closed the outside door but actually he hid behind the door and watched her. She was angry and yelled to be released, cursing and trying desperately to untie the ropes, pleading to end the game. With renewed arousal, Ted watched her stunning naked body moving violently, trying desperately to get free.

After about ten minutes, he entered the room smiling. "You wanted to play the dominance game. Well you got it."

"This is not funny Ted. The game is over. Untie me right away," she said angrily.

"You said everything goes."

"Stop it. It's not funny."

He ignored her plea, undressed and entered her again. At first, she protested but quickly plunged back into the game, enjoying the twist of trickery Ted had played on her.

"Are you sure you're not too drunk?" Heather pulled him from his reverie.

"I'm almost there," Ted said, returning to the erotic memory with Lindsey, increasing his rhythm and, with faster strokes, yelled as he climaxed. Then, Ted rolled over and fell into a deep sleep. Frustrated, Heather covered Ted with a blanket and hugged his back, trying to capture through his warm body the absence of his attention.

16

The twelfth of January proved to be a bad-weather choice for a trial date.

Freezing snow and sleet brought on by a northwestern storm made the journey to the courthouse very difficult. Streets were covered with ice, and the city trucks worked overtime to spray salt mixed with sand to help make them passable. "The show must go on," was the message from Judge Boyd, to those callers checking to see if the trial was being postponed. "Everyone must show up." She wanted it understood that she was not going to drag the trial out any longer than necessary.

Ted was eager the whole weekend. On Monday morning he woke at four o'clock, took a shower, and chose his clothes for the day. He wore a light blue shirt, with a white trimmed collar that was a perfect setting for his designer print tie, all wrapped up by a black sheen suit. Satisfied with his selection, he sat down at his desk to enjoy his coffee. He had asked Heather not to wake up with him so he could have the morning to himself. He needed this time before delivering his opening statement to put his thoughts in order.

The State of New York vs. Elliot Barrett was printed on the top of the thick file prepared and arranged in perfect in sequence on his desk. From past experience he knew that the opening statement was the most important first impression in the jury's conclusion of guilt or innocence. Some research studies report say sixty percent of the jurors make up their minds the first day and carry those same opinions until the end of the trial. He felt confident his arguments would be sufficient to instill enough doubt in the jurors to win this circumstantial evidence case. *I can't make too many mistakes with George around; he is getting better and better*, Ted thought.

Looking through the window at the fast falling snow, he saw that Central Park was covered with snow, and the water reservoir frozen to ice. Only a few people walked on paths usually crowded with activity. The evergreen trees were the only punctuation of color on the white ground. He turned to the local news forecast and decided to leave early to arrive at the courtroom on time. Once on the road he regretted that he decided to drive, but carefully managed to maneuver slowly on the icy streets.

Elliot and Ruth ordered a limousine to drive them to the courthouse. They were hesitant to drive with so much ice on the road. Along the road they saw many sliding cars. Elliot's face was pale and his strained body reflected his psyche. "This must end soon," Elliot murmured. "I hate it. I just want my life back." Ruth looked at him tenderly and hugged him, feeling his tense body. "Do you know what I mean? A man gets up one morning, and his life has been turned upside down. Life can be so fragile. Look at all the accidents on the road out there; in one moment a life can change forever."

"Hey, don't be so gloomy," Ruth scorned lightly. "Life is also beautiful. We are going to get past this hurdle and get our lives back. Maybe there is a lesson we can learn from all this. Maybe God is testing us and there is a purpose we don't understand yet."

Elliot was not encouraged by Ruth's words and couldn't bring himself to join in her optimistic outlook. "There are all kinds of things that can go wrong."

"We must think positive. We must be strong," Ruth insisted.

There are too many lessons I have learned already, Elliot thought. *A few I wish I could go back and redo. A few I cannot restore. Some I wish I never got into in the first place.*

They arrived half an hour early and found Ted already there. The Criminal Courts Building at 100 Centre Street is located near the Brooklyn Bridge, one of the grand buildings making up the

Civic Center. Elliot was intimidated when he entered through the huge guard towers, great Babylonian slabs of granite that gave the building an awesome presence. Ted referred to it as 'The Tombs,' because of the deathly conditions of the city jail contained inside.

Ted's energetic welcome restored some of Elliot's spirit. Ted was pleased at their proper dress. Elliot was dressed conservatively. Ruth wore a purple-and-pink flowered outfit that made her look like a good Texas girl. *Usually I can't stand how she dresses but for this purpose she looks great for the jury*, Ted thought.

"What an awful morning," Elliot said.

"It's a great morning. Forget about the weather. We need every ounce of energy concentrated on the trial," Ted responded. They sat in the lounge and Ted gave a quick briefing of the day's proceedings, and last minute instructions of behavior necessary to impress the jury. They went through the evidence and all the possible explanations of each allegation. Ted repeated that Elliot did not have to testify at all in the trial, but he could reserve that option. "The burden of proof rests solely with the prosecutor."

At five minutes to ten they entered the courtroom. On the door a sign was posted in capital letters, N.Y. v ELLIOT BARRETT. There was a different feeling in the courtroom than there had been at the preliminary proceeding. Everything seemed much more demanding. The jury of eight women and four men, including six African-Americans, seemed attentive. Judge Boyd ruled with an iron fist. She did not show favor to either side. The large symbol hanging on the wall—the blindfolded woman holding the balance scale that symbolized fairness and objectivity—could have been Judge Boyd. The American flag hung in the back corner of the courtroom, as if overseeing that everything would be done legally.

Ted noticed that even George rose to the occasion and wore a dark suit with a white shirt, but his tie was wider and shorter than it should have been. *George couldn't help it, but he definitely should get some credit for his effort*, Ted thought, amused.

Everyone was waiting anxiously for the moment when Judge

Boyd would bang the gavel to start the proceedings. After entering the courtroom, she looked sternly at Elliot, requesting his plea of guilt or innocence. There was complete silence in the room as Elliot stood up to enter a plea. His pale face, showed enormous pressure despite Ted's instructions to look relaxed. In a quiet, steady voice he said "Not guilty." Ruth felt pain in her chest following Elliot's statement. *How can it be that such a good and innocent man be charged and wrongfully accused? Why did he deserve all this?*

Judge Boyd observed Elliot intently, trying to measure his statement through her experienced eyes. She noticed Ruth and felt compassion for what she would have to endure throughout the long proceedings.

George decided to adapt the same strategy he had used successfully in the preliminary proceeding. In his opening statement he stressed the main points of his argument. To establish a romantic link between Elliot and Lindsey, to establish physical evidence that tied Elliot to the crime scene and to establish a motive. He talked directly to the jury with tranquil but firm conviction. He would prove, beyond a reasonable doubt, that on the night of the twenty-eighth of September, between nine thirty and eleven P.M., Elliot was welcomed into Lindsey's apartment. In the course of the evening a fight broke out and Elliot pushed Lindsey, where resulted in her falling and hitting her head on the wooden arm of the couch and momentarily losing consciousness. While he tightly held her wrists above her head, he used the pillow as a weapon and killed Lindsey by suffocation. George explained the details of ach phase, point by point with razor-sharp clarity.

Damn good opening statement, Ted thought as he got up for his turn.

"Your Honor, ladies and gentlemen of the jury," Ted's charming, smooth voice cut the silence in the courtroom. He pointed toward Elliot. "In front of you sits an innocent man tragically accused of a crime he didn't commit. Dr. Elliot Barrett, a renowned physician, is in the business of saving lives. As a matter of fact, we are going to invite as one of our witnesses, and I repeat our witness, not the prosecutor's witness, Ms. Margaret Anderson the mother of the deceased, Ms. Lindsey Anderson. She will testify that Dr. Barrett saved her life. She will testify that she has the highest regard for Dr. Barrett and that her daughter spoke positively of him. She will testify that she did not see, hear or think that Dr. Barrett was involved with her daughter romantically."

Ted turned toward George's team and pointed his finger. "As they would like you to believe," he said in a dramatic tone. "As a matter of fact, not even once did Lindsey mention Elliot to her mother in any romantic context." Ted pointed again toward George. "As they would like you to believe," he repeated. "We will prove beyond a shadow of a doubt that Dr. Barrett was professional and caring, as a matter of fact, maybe more caring than duty called for, which might have placed him in this situation." Ted explained Elliot's unique ongoing involvement with Lindsey as a friendly doctor-patient relationship. He explained the existence of the physical evidence as a result of Elliot's visit to care for his patient.

Ted paused, creating a long dramatic silence. All eyes in the courtroom were glued on him. His manipulative displays of drama played skillfully to the jury. He cleared his throat and continued. "We are also going to prove that the preponderance of evidence the prosecutor wants you to believe is not factual but circumstantial." Then with a loud voice, as if warning the crowd, he stated, "I will prove how the rush to judgment and the sloppy workmanship of the police and the investigating team have dragged an innocent man to this needless trial.

"They would have you believe that what they say are facts, but in actuality, it's just a theory. It sounds good, but it does not have any roots in truth. We will show beyond any shadow of a doubt that the crime was not committed by Dr. Barrett." He stood in silence looking first at the jury as if to let them digest his words, then turning to George. Having finished his performance, he sat down at his desk.

Elliot thought Ted's opening statement was effective. Ruth

agreed. George now knew what kind of strategy Ted would be using during the trial.

To everyone's surprise, the jury was dismissed early due to the worsening weather. After stating instructions to the jury on their conduct, Judge Boyd repeated her instructions not to arrive at any conclusions and not to speak to jury members.

"All rise," was the familiar call of the courtroom clerk. Everyone stood as the judge left the courtroom.

17

What happened outside of the courtroom took Ruth and Elliot by surprise.

They were shocked by the swarm of newspaper and local television reporters awaiting them at the courthouse entry. Camera lights flashed in their faces and they were bombarded with questions. The reporters shoved microphones in their faces and demanded answers to their questions. Ruth held Elliot's hand tightly, and felt his trembling hand pressing back.

Ted took charge of the situation, using experience from former encounters with the media to aid in answering questions firmly. "At this early phase, we only have a short statement to make. We feel good about our opening statement. Dr. Barrett is innocent and the truth will come to light." The reporters were unrelenting. They blocked their path to the street, yelling in chaos.

"Is Elliot going to testify?" a reported asked.

"Please excuse me," Ted pushed his way to the exit, smiling at the reporters, knowing full well how important it was to rally the media behind his case. "We need to be on the road before the road conditions get worse. I promise we will have more to say soon."

Ted, Elliot and Ruth managed to push through the crowd of reporters and disappeared into the waiting limousine. The driver took off and drove Ted to the parking lot where he had parked his car.

"I was not prepared for that," Elliot said, still pale from the experience.

"Yes Ted, you should have warned us," Ruth said angrily.

"You cannot be prepared. You have to go through the fire. I told you there would be reporters asking questions," Ted said.

"I know. You're right. It was too sudden…too overwhelming," Ruth said, still shivering from the cold and the experience.

"Guys, tomorrow George's direct questioning will begin and we must be ready."

Ted tried to escape Ruth stare. "Let's get home before the ice makes driving impossible."

Before the trial started Elliot was very concerned about the impact of the publicity on his life. He asked Ted if he had the ability to legally prevent it from happening. Ted explained that was practically impossible. In a pre-trial motion with Judge Boyd, he and George had expressed their views about the publicity issue.

Ted argued that pre-trial publicity would prevent his client from getting a fair trial. He argued that Elliot was a prominent member of the community and adverse publicity might prejudice potential jurors. Furthermore, he argued the media has its main motivation to create drama to attract larger ratings to sensationalize the trial. He feared that the media might disclose evidence, and that they might create an inflammatory picture that could influence potential jurors to feel negatively toward Elliot.

George felt that defending the right of the public to know was of utmost importance. He argued that even in the case of a juror having a prior opinion or information on the case, the opinion would be put aside.

Judge Boyd, in a lengthy opinion, denied Ted's motion. In her thorough explanation, she pointed out that a city the size of New York had no problem finding plenty of jurors. Though the crime might contain gossip, it was not so inflammatory and the accused was not such a famous figure as to create a public outcry. She maintained the right of the public to know, as protected by the constitution. Only on rare occasions, when a juror might have presumptive prejudice against the defendant, might the service of a juror be denied. In addition she felt she was more than fair by not allowing

TV coverage in the courtroom.

On the drive home from the courthouse the driver turned left on FDR Drive. Elliot could not recapture the sense of freedom he had felt when Ted had driven him home after his dreadful night in jail. He looked through the window of the limo at the empty street and felt his own emptiness and loneliness. The East River was gray like the sky above, and the grace of the Brooklyn Bridge failed to soothe his soul. As they drove by the Fulton Fish Market the strong smells nauseated him.

Even with Ruth's supporting love, Elliot felt he was sinking deeper into a sense of anguish that stifled his psyche. He was losing his ability to lift himself out of the abyss. He sank into the limousine seat, closed his eyes and tried to forget his misery. Ruth placed his head on her shoulder. Her kindness increased his sense of shame and isolation, and he was engulfed with guilt.

The next day in the courtroom, George began his direct line of questioning of witnesses. Ted would follow with his cross examination, followed by George's examination each man trying to convince the jurors that his argument was the right one.

At times, the arguments grew feisty. Judge Boyd called them to the sidebar and threatened to hold them in contempt of court.

Ted did not make the same mistake as he had the preliminary hearing. This time, he was more careful when questioning Patricia, the waitress. But George scored a point by strengthening the credibility of her testimony about Elliot and Lindsey being intimately involved. She repeated her testimony that she was certain of Elliot's identity because she had a crush on him. As had happened before, there was much laughter in the courtroom. Judge Boyd, however, was not amused. She warned the attendees she would clear the courtroom if there were more disturbances.

On cross, Ted wanted to get the same result with the waitress as in the preliminary hearing. He wanted to discredit George. "You said in your previous testimony that the defendant and Elliot were a little more than friendly."

"I don't quite remember what I said a few months ago at the hearing," Patricia said.

"No problem. Your Honor, I would like to refresh the witness's memory. Here on page number thirty-eight in the copy of your previous testimony, line number six," he pointed at Patricia. "Can you find the line?"

"Yes sir."

Ted started reading from the manuscript. "And I am quoting: Question: You said they were very friendly. Were they holding hands?"

"No sir."

"Were they kissing?"

"No sir."

Ted paused for a moment to sip his water and to see if he had the attention of the jury. He then continued his reading. "Question: So you say they were simply friendly but not romantic?"

"Well, a little more than just friendly."

"A little more. Did you hear any of their conversation?"

"No sir."

"Then it's just your opinion, not actual fact that you can state for certain."

"That's correct sir; that's what I felt from what I observed."

Ted put the transcript down. "Now, did this refresh your memory?" Ted looked directly at Patricia.

"Yes sir."

"Earlier in the day, when George asked you about the nature of the encounter, you said they were intimate. Didn't we already establish they were only a little friendly?"

"Objection," George said.

"Overruled. Please answer the question," Judge Boyd said.

Patricia seemed a little confused and looked at George for help. "I felt they were friendly enough."

"Your Honor, no more questions." Ted had gotten what he wanted.

George followed, as he had in the preliminary proceedings with the same order and line of questioning of Arnold Blumenthal, who testified that he had seen a Mercedes similar to Elliot's on the night of the murder.

Ted was prepared when his time came to cross-examine the witness. "You testified today and also previously that you saw a Mercedes on the night in question?" Ted carefully set up his trap.

"Yes sir."

"Did you by any chance manage to see the license plate number?" Ted asked, knowing this time not to be surprised.

"No sir."

"Can you tell the jury, how can you be certain of the exact specifications of the car?"

"Yes sir," he said gladly. "I own a '96 Mercedes and stopped to admire the new model, the 500SL."

"Okay. So you saw the car parked next to your shop, and you say you recognized the year and the model. Can you tell what color it was?"

"Yes, it was black."

"So you are sure it was a '97 model?"

"Yes, I already testified…"

"And you are sure it was a 500SL model…?

"Objection, he already answered that," George said. *Where is he going with these established facts?* He thought.

"Can we move on?" Judge Boyd ordered.

Ted nodded. "Are you sure it was black?"

Before another objection was called, Mr. Blumenthal answered with raised eyebrows. "Yes sir I'm sure it was black…"

"For the record, Defense Exhibit number twenty, admitted to evidence." Ted had a little smile whenever he was ready to strike the final blow. "Your Honor, may I approach the witness?" He waited for the formal response.

"You may."

"Is this similar to the car you saw?"

"Yes, yes sir. Just like the car I saw."

"Can you tell the members of the jury the color of the car?"

Mr. Blumenthal looked intently at the picture. "It's the same model… but this car is dark blue."

"What if I tell you this is Elliot's car…"

"Objection."

"Overruled."

George realized he had not paid close attention to this detail. He realized that at ten o'clock on a dark street the color might be perceived as black. In the re-cross he tried desperately to correct the impression and stressed the point that it was dark that night, but the damage was already done. He knew there were only a few cars of this model on the streets, and that it was probably Elliot's car. But the witness had testified that he saw a black car. The accused had a dark-blue car. That is what would remain in the jury's minds.

Ted felt he had planted a sense of doubt in the jury's members of the jury and established a weaker link than George had tried to portray. He saw the surprise on George's face when Mr. Blumenthal was confused about the color. He noticed that the jurors were interested in his line of questioning and paid attention as he steered them skillfully to where he wanted them to go. Elliot seemed encouraged and Ruth's face seemed quietly delighted.

I was doing so well up to this point, George thought. Ted looked at George and showed him three fingers, in a way only both would recognize, as if saying 'Three for me, two for you.'

18

The trial started to gain coverage in the media. At first it was only local newspapers and television stations that reported the facts and added dramatic flavor. They reported about the respected Manhattanites' love triangle, a wealthy couple, a SoHo gallery owner, and the renowned doctor who was accused of killing the daughter of his patient whose life he had saved.

As news coverage increased, a few of Lindsey's friends came forth and added fuel to the fire. Coverage was devoted to her flamboyant personality, her wild lifestyle and her many lovers. When a national court television network started to cover the story, more national news syndicates also followed suit.

The media coverage became more gossipy, reporting in detail about the life of the mild-mannered Elliot and his devoted wife. Some reported on Margaret, abandoned by her husband for a younger woman, twenty-four years earlier. In spite of growing pressure from the district attorney's office Lindsey's mother strongly believed in her doctor. But as the trial progressed, the story started to take on a different turn as someone from the district attorney's office started leaking information anonymously.

One tabloid started a rumor of a long history of marital problems between Elliot and Ruth. Another came up with a fabricated story about Elliot's cold and indifferent attitude toward his staff and patients. A reporter found an article about Elliot's view of terminal patients and ways to treat them, and created the distorted view that Elliot supported mercy killing in extreme cases of illness.

One tabloid reported that there were a few malpractice suits pending against his clinic without checking to see that Elliot had no personal involvement in any of them. Ruth was enraged when a tabloid reporter tried to interview her children.

She had to calm down Caroline, who found the unwanted attention very hard to deal with. She wanted to quit school and stay at home, saying the pressure to study was too difficult. Caroline asked difficult questions about Elliot's innocence and wanted to know, in view of all she heard on the television, if she had been told the whole truth. Ruth explained that the media was sensationalizing the story. Although Jonathan seemed to handle the situation better, Ruth knew that he kept his feelings inside and he was also experiencing pain. She managed to convince both of them that the best course of action was to hold on to a normal life as much as possible and to seek the inner strength to help them to get past this dreadful situation. She expressed her full confidence in Elliot's innocence and urged them to trust that the truth would come to light with Elliot's acquittal from all charges.

Ruth found herself explaining and defending Elliot to friends who called after they read the news or watched the television coverage. She heard the doubt in their voices as they discussed the case. Many believed that there must be some truth to the stories, or media sources could not be permitted to print or air them. Ruth explained that she could go to court and sue to prove the lies, but was not going to do so on order to avoid increasing attention from the media. She felt frustrated because nothing could be done to stop them from publishing based on conjecture or rumor.

Ted decided to combat the rumors with fact. At first Eliot was reluctant, fearful of more invasion of his privacy. But Ruth realized it must be done. She explained to Elliot that otherwise the rumors would not stop and people would believe the lies. Before calling a news conference, Ted drilled Elliot and Ruth on potential questions reporters would ask and they rehearsed possible responses. Ruth spoke about her wonderful husband. She begged the reporters to leave her children out of the public eye. Elliot said that the attacks on his family had hurt him deeply and affected his children. They both spoke of their happy life together and Elliot described his work as a physician. Ted added that the case was undermining "an innocent man, falsely accused."

Ted decided to take advantage of the news coverage to attack the police.

"The police, right from the beginning, like horses with blinders on, focused on one possibility and refused to consider other potential suspects." Ted decided to exploit Lindsey's life style to the media, but was reluctant to bring this matter before the court. He claimed that this circumstantial case would result in an acquittal. Ted wanted to gain the public's sympathy, which knew would help his case.

The next day Judge Boyd called both Ted and George to her chamber. "I want to understand what is going on," she demanded coldly. "Why is my case being tried in the media?"

"We don't have any choice in the matter," Ted said. "We had to respond to the smearing and inflammatory rumors coming from the D.A.'s office. We had to present our side."

"I have no knowledge of anyone leaking anything," George snapped.

"This must stop. I mean both of you must stop," Judge Boyd said. She gave a threatening look to George, then to Ted. "Understood?"

"If they stop, we…." Ted began to say.

"I don't want to discuss any of this again. If I get the impression that any side is breaking my rules, there will be severe consequences. The only thing I will approve is a daily statement from both sides. If that doesn't work, we'll stop even that," she looked at them severely. "You must submit your statements to my office, at the end of each day. Only after my approval, can they be released without any deviations. Is that clear?"

Outside of Judge Boyd's chamber George and Ted felt like students by a professor. "Cranky Granny was really cranky today,"

George said. "She was close to demanding a gag order."

"Seriously George, you should control your staff. Someone is leaking information to the press."

"I'm going to. I promise, someone is going to get his head chopped off today. I don't like this kind of play. It is not fair to your client."

"I suppose we both have to subtract one point from each other's score," Ted said, smiling.

"Let me see where we stand at this moment. You mean four for me and zero for you?" George laughed.

"Not on your life. It's standing at three for me, two for you."

"I was just kidding. I see you are really keeping score." George tapped Ted's shoulder affectionately. "I'll see you in court tomorrow."

"See you tomorrow."

During the next few days, George moved on to his next line of questioning. He knew that he would be presenting his strongest evidence. The presence of physical evidence at Lindsey's place linked Elliot to the crime scene. He called uniformed police followed by detectives to the witness stand. They described the crime scene and evidence they had found. Forensic analysis of Elliot of the actual physical evidence linked Elliot to the crime scene.

George's main witness was Homicide Detective Sills. "The people call Detective Benjamin Sills," George said dramatically.

Sills was sworn in by Judge Boyd. "Raise your right hand please. You do solemnly swear that the testimony you give in the case now pending before the court, shall be the truth, the whole truth and nothing but the truth, so help you God."

"I do."

"Please be seated in the witness stand and state and spell your first and last name for the record."

George questioned Sills about his qualifications and impressive record with the police before getting into his description of the crime scene.

"Can you tell the jury," George asked, "where the fingerprints were found?"

"Yes, they were found in many places in the living room, and also on the bathroom mirror."

"You said bathroom, as in her personal bedroom?" George wanted Sills to clarify his answer for the jury.

"Yes sir."

"Were there any fingerprints in the living room?"

"Most of the fingerprints were found on the couch," Detective Sills gestured to a diagram of the layout of the apartment.

"You mean the couch where she was found dead?"

"Yes sir."

George asked a few more technical questions about the fingerprints, and then asked about the hair samples.

"The hair samples were found in proximity to the same places as the fingerprints." Sills explained.

George gave Sills the telephone records and asked if her telephone calls were made to Elliot. The high number of telephone calls had struck Sills early in the investigation and pointed to Elliot's guilt.

Ruth was surprised when she heard that there were sixty-five calls in seven months. *I must ask Elliot about these calls*, she thought.

Elliot hadn't realized that the total would be so high. He knew Ruth would question him about the calls on the way home.

Ted had prepared some plausible explanations, hoping to turn the evidence to his advantage. He planned to make a connection to Margaret's testimony about the personal and excellent care Elliot had provided to her.

"Four calls in March." Detective Sills continued his answer. "Four in April. Eight in May. Ten calls in June. Twelve in July. Twelve in August and fifteen calls placed in October," Sills counted methodically.

"Would you consider this a large volume of calls?" George asked, wanting to plant that question in the minds of the jury.

"Objection. It's not his area of expertise," Ted said.

"Overruled."

"Okay, I withdraw the question. Did you note that there were fewer calls in the first three months than in the last three months?"

Detective Sills said he had, and came to the conclusion that there was more need for communication in the last three months because in his estimation the romance had gathered momentum. He said that he recalled questioning Mrs. Anderson during his investigation, and that she said she was in increasingly better health after the month of August. "I saw no reason why the calls became more frequent, unless they were personal."

19

Ted was not surprised by Detective Sills's testimony, which increased the complexities of the case. Elliott did not know that Ted knew of his affair with Lindsey. Ted knew that she had dated married men before and always she was careful to call her lovers at their work place. She made her calls to Elliot from her gallery telephone on the first floor. Other times, she would leave messages on their beepers and wait for her lovers to call back. Apparently, the police had not checked her business telephone records where calls would be found. Since Elliot was her mother's doctor, Lindsey must have felt that she didn't have to take her usual precautions.

Ted wanted to direct the attention away from the strong forensic experts George was going to call. He did not want to get into lengthy technical arguments that would bore the jury. His tactic was to concede the existence of physical evidence found in Lindsey's apartment on frequent occasions. He agreed with George's assumption that Elliot was in the apartment at times. He wanted to establish that Elliot was there because he came to see his patient.

Ted asked Sills, "You testified before that you had no knowledge of the content of the conversations between Dr. Barrett and Ms. Lindsey Anderson."

"No sir," Detective Sills answered calmly.

"Were any calls placed to his residence?"

"No, only to his clinic but ..."

"Please, answer only what is being asked," Ted said. "Do you know how many calls were made by Mrs. Margaret Anderson, the mother?"

Detective Sills was not expecting this question. "No…but we can …"

"Please, Your Honor, instruct the witness to answer only what I asked."

"No sir," Sills said, responding to the judge's instruction.

"Okay, now about the fingerprints. You testified they were found on the mirror in the bedroom bathroom?"

"Yes sir."

"Did the police check to see what was behind the mirror?"

"Only a regular medicine cabinet."

"Did you check if some of the medicine belonged to Mrs. Margaret Anderson? Yes or no?"

"What the…" Sills tried to reply.

"Please answer yes or no to my questions," Ted wanted to corner Sills.

"No," Sills answered tersely.

"What if Dr. Barrett was there to check the medicine Margaret was taking?" Ted said pointedly.

"Objection."

George and Sills knew that this line of questioning challenged the competency of the police. George asked for the judge's confirmation. "Your Honor, this is all speculation," George said to the judge. "This was not in the discovery." Ted explained that later Mrs. Anderson would testify on that issue and show a connection to this line of questioning. The judge allowed him to continue.

"Were any calls made on the day of the crime, yes or no?" Ted continued.

"No sir."

"O.K. let's move on to another question." Ted liked using the technique going back and forth and confusing the witness's train of thought. He wanted to question Sills about the location of the hair, and then go back to the calls, but Sills would not budge and answered calmly. He was a terrible witness for a defense lawyer. It was impossible to distract him.

George continued his redirect for a few hours, eliciting more information from the reliable detective. He knew that stressing the point that Elliot was seen with Lindsey outside of the apartment as well as the existence of the physical evidence in the apartment would raise questions for the jury. He wished all of his witnesses could be so easy to work with. He had worked in the past with Sills and held him in high regard.

On re-cross, Ted tried to push Sills' buttons. He wanted to show the jury that this calm man was using a clever demeanor. Sills was really a cunning, tough detective. "So, you said you hadn't checked thoroughly a few of the points we mentioned before? Is there anything else you want to tell the jury which you haven't checked yet?"

Sills' face grew red; Ted's question triggered a scornful response. "I'm a civil servant; I'm not anyone's enemy. We put our lives on the line. I'm here to describe what I have observed with the knowledge and experience gained over thirty-five years of service." Agitated, he continued over Ted's objection. "I will not have my name smeared and my integrity challenged by you or by anyone."

Ted gained partially what he wanted and asked the judge to strike the damaging remark from the record. Judge Boyd looked at Ted, as if saying 'You asked for it, you got it.' She instructed the jury to ignore Sills' comments and told him to answer only the questions asked. Ted and Sills both knew that such statements could influence a jury.

George relied on physical evidence to make a strong connection to the crime scene. Forensic technicians were called to the witness stand to explain each article that was found at the crime scene, which established Elliot at the crime scene. Ted again proposed that the physical evidence had been there for months. He argued that it was not placed there on the night of the crime. George, with a sarcastic tone, dismissed Ted's arguments as weak excuses to deny actual facts.

George knew that, in the mind of spectators present in a courtroom, even a gruesome crime scene can be far removed from the severity of its actual reality. He needed to create a drama to show that a real person had been murdered. George had the ability to direct the questions with a systematic, clear-line sequence, creating a coherent picture for the jury to follow, like pieces of a puzzle. George again placed Lindsey's photographs in evidence. He connected the VCR to the television monitor, knowing the effectiveness of this kind of presentation. He knew that statistics showed that the average person spent over six hours in front of the television each day and is used to receiving information that way. He showed a computer animation video dramatizing of what he proposed happened on the night of the murder.

The jury was glued to the monitor as the murder scene came alive onscreen. They could see the apartment layout and how Lindsey was pushed forcefully, hitting the chair and falling on the couch. It showed the assailant, supposedly Elliot, hovering over her body, holding her hands over her head and suffocating her with the pillow.

George replayed parts of the video as he questioned of medical examiner. "You testified under oath in front of the jury that Lindsey was pushed, hit the back of her head on the couch and was suffocated by a couch pillow." George set up the groundwork for his questioning.

"Yes sir. The autopsy concluded it was a murder."

"Explain to the jury how that was determined."

Dr. Rajastan explained, in a lengthy and detailed presentation that included diagrams, his examination of the deceased's brain and how he could determine the flow of blood to the brain and how it affected the function of the physical brain and eyes.

"And are you certain that the time of death was between 9:30 and 12:00 PM.?"

"Yes sir," he said, and proceeded to give a lengthy explanation of the rationale behind his conclusion. "We call it 'the range of time of death' and it's determined by the autopsy. We check the gastric contents and its character; we observe the rigor mortis, lividity, temperature of the liver and rate of change and eye fluids."

George continued his questioning for a few more hours, going through each detail of the facts. Dr. Rajastan gave his answers in a laconic voice but George kept up the emotion.

Ruth was not interested in the lengthy, dull testimony of the forensic doctor but Elliot followed it closely and passed notes to Ted commenting on the testimony. At the end of direct, Ted felt George had managed to create a clear and convincing argument. He knew he had to remove some strong impressions in the jury's minds. He knew exactly how the murder had happened. Throughout the testimony he was astonished at how wrong the detective and the coroner were about some of their assumptions. He had to find a way to cross examine witnesses without revealing how much he actually knew. Elliot passed a note to Ted concerning the source of the food content and the high level of alcohol found in Lindsey's stomach. He wanted Ted to argue that point. Ted felt cornered since he knew about the source, but felt he must follow Elliot's suggestions. The police had not investigated that point and Ted was afraid of drawing attention to that detail. He was afraid to open a Pandora 's Box that would create a trail leading to him, to their dining together and had fun out on the town during the last six months. With the attendant media publicity, someone could come forth and connect him to Lindsey's death.

"You testified that the body was found two days after its death, Dr. Rajastan?"

"Yes, approximately forty-four hours to be exact."

"Was the body in a condition to make such an accurate prediction?"

"Yes, it's pretty scientific nowadays. We can determine the degrading factor of a body."

"Okay, can you then tell me when the food content found in her stomach was eaten?"

"Yes, we can say with certain accuracy that it was eaten approximately two hours before her death."

"With this kind of accuracy, can you identify the source of the food?"

Dr. Rajastan was confused. "No sir, you mean what restaurant…, no. We can determine if it was Thai or Chinese food, if that's what you mean. Also, it was red wine but we cannot determine what kind of wine or where it came from."

"We will get back to that issue later on. You testified that the deceased had struggled with her assailant. Did you find any physical evidence on her body to indicate struggles?"

"No."

"Under her fingernails?"

"No."

"So you theorized that she was fighting with someone but did not touch the assailant. How about kicking, scratching?"

"No sir."

"How then did you conclude she was fighting back?"

"Someone had to restrain her. There were marks on her wrists."

"Yes the blue marks. I understand. But you say there was a fight. You say she fought back?" Ted pressed harder.

"I don't know the nature of the fight but there was some sort of struggle."

"Now, you say there was a struggle. Before you testified there was fighting." Ted flashed that little smile again.

"Okay, it was a struggle," Dr. Rajastan conceded.

"You testified under oath before the jury that you do not know the source of the food. And now you say it was not a fight? Are you changing your testimony, Dr. Rajastan?"

"Objection. He is putting words in the witness's mouth," George said.

"Overruled."

Ted felt he was stretching the line and entering into dangerous territory that might hurt him, but felt compelled to continue. He had lost the preliminary preceding and feared it was because he didn't get deep enough to the bottom of each issue in order to create doubt in the jurors' minds.

"You testified that a pillow was used to suffocate. Then, in previous testimony, you agreed to the possibility that death could have happened accidentally if her head had ended up face down in the pillow. She could have suffocated herself."

"If I remember correctly, it was asked as a hypothetical question. As far as I know from my observation of the crime scene, the head was found face up. There was a slight possibility it could have happened the way you presented it. I maintain, with high probability, she was suffocated manually with the pillow."

"As far as you know that's right. But you do not know."

"The picture showed…"

"Yes, the photograph. Only if her head was facing up. Can you say with complete certainty…"

"Objection. Too many questions. He won't let the witness finish his answers," George complained.

"Yes, please be simple. One question at a time," Judge Boyd ruled.

"Is it fair to say it was only probable?" Ted pushed his point.

"Highly probable. As you know, police are not allowed to touch the body; only the coroner is allowed," Dr. Rajastan insisted.

"Do you actually know what happened before you arrived at the crime scene?"

"No sir."

Ted continued to push his agenda to create a picture of uncertainty. He was planning to pursue this line of questioning with Detective Sills. He would grill him about all the things he did not investigate thoroughly enough.

George suspected Ted was trying to establish the death was not a murder but an accident. Ted's line of questioning pointed to the possibility that there was no actual struggle. By doing so, Ted could promote the theory that Lindsay was drunk, fell down on her face, and had died from lack of air. *Very clever*, George thought, *but it won't work. Maybe Ted is also trying to create a scenario to protect his client from a charge of first-degree murder? The photograph clearly showed Lindsey lying face up. Is he going to try to confuse Margaret into admitting that she touched the body and tampered with the evidence when she first saw her daughter?*

George typed a note to himself to investigate that point. He added a note about the source of the food content found in the stomach. Sills had not investigated the source of the food. There was no evidence of a container left in the apartment to show that food was brought in from outside. He typed another note to investigate whether some evidence could have been removed by the assailant. He remembered that only Lindsey's fingerprints were found on the wine bottle. He admired the insight and ingenuity Ted had shown with other possibilities, but felt that his chances of conviction were still holding strong.

20

After the lunch recess Ted continued questioning Dr. Rajastan. He wanted to come up with a few other plausible scenarios for Lindsey's death. He knew from previously questioning of jurors after trials that this would create more confusion in the jury. They would not perceive the prosecutor's scenario as the only possibility, and Ted's scenario would be regarded as a probable theory.

Elliot did not understand exactly where Ted's line of questioning was heading. But he felt that by creating confusion Ted was a constructing a good line of defense.

"How many glasses of wine did the deceased have at the time of her death?" Ted asked Dr. Rajastan.

"Two to three glasses of wine in the course of the evening."

"In your opinion, was she legally drunk?"

"No, I do not think so…"

"You are talking about legally drunk or being in a state of drunkenness?" Ted asked.

"I am talking about being legally drunk."

"So you do not know to what degree she was impaired that night, do you?"

"I can theorize…"

"Yes or no. Dr. Rajastan," Ted pressed.

"No… not how …"

"That's all I need," Ted said abruptly. "Now, being under the influence, couldn't the deceased have fallen backward and hit her head without outside influence?"

"Oh no. She had to be pushed hard to get the kind of injury

she had at the back of her head."

Ted decided to risk what he knew really happened. "The chair was broken, wasn't it?"

"Yes it was."

"Was it possible that the deceased stumbled into the chair and fell down sideways, very hard?" Ted demonstrated the movement. "In that case, wouldn't her wounds be as serious as you describe?"

"In my estimation, someone had to push her to create her wounds."

"No more questions."

George immediately wanted to emphasize Dr. Rajastan's assurance. He got up energetically and asked Khalil, "Is it fair to say, you are completely ruling out the possibility of an accident?"

"Yes. There was someone else involved in her death."

"No more questions."

That evening when Ted was flipping his remote control from station to station, he could not believe the many interpretations of what was happening in the courtroom. Opinion was split among the TV commentators. Some maintained that after a solid direct from George's excellent performance, Ted was preparing an elegant retreat into admittance of guilt, but only as an accident. Others maintained it was an excellent defense performance that would yield a surprise result at the end of final arguments. One expert said that Ted's insistence on Lindsey's intoxicated condition opened the possibility that she had not been murdered.

In a statement to the press, Ted pleaded with them to stop speculating and wait until his direct showed where his line of questioning would lead. He reaffirmed his client's innocence and his commitment to complete acquittal.

Ruth was watching coverage of the trial when the telephone rang. "Hello Ruth. How are you?"

"Hopefully it will get better, Mr. Barrett."

"Have you being watching the television? All this media coverage is just unbelievable," he said angrily. "Is Elliot there?"

"No, he's at the clinic trying to hold on to some continuity."

"Well, good, I actually wanted to talk to you. Ruth, I am asking, for Elliot's sake, can we keep a secret between us?"

"What secrets are...?" Ruth hesitated.

"Hear me out. What I want to say is very important. Elliot has been acting strangely since this mess started. You know, Ruth, we only want the best for him. Recently, for no reason, he's started to be stubborn like a child and doesn't want to hear any advice..."

They always say it's for the good of their children even when they're really concerned with themselves, Ruth thought. "Don't you think Elliot can make decisions for himself?" Ruth was intent on defending her husband.

"Well, fine, but he found the wrong time not to listen to some good common sense."

Ruth thought that Elliot's emotional connection to his father was a bit oppressive, but left it alone. When Elliot wanted to return to Boston to establish his clinic after finishing his residency, she convinced him to stay in Manhattan. She felt even then that Elliot's parents were too involved in their lives. She thought that physical distance would help them gain enough freedom to build a life of their own.

"What good advice?" Ruth asked.

"After he lost in the preliminary hearing, I told Elliot it would be a good idea to get my lawyer to join the team and help Ted. I wanted ... the secret I want you to know... actually I wanted you to help me convince Elliot it's still not too late."

"What is your secret?" Ruth tried to understand.

"I will tell you, but promise me that if you do not agree, this stays between us."

"Okay. I promise," Ruth said reluctantly.

"Since the beginning of the trial I have been speaking to a good friend of mine, an excellent criminal lawyer, Saul Bernstein. On my behalf, he sent one of his assistants to follow the proceedings and report first-hand what was going on in the courtroom."

"Who is he?" Ruth was surprised.

"He is sitting a few rows in the back, not far from where you sit."

"Where the guests are seated? I didn't pay any…"

"Anyway, Ruth, yesterday I met with Mr. Bernstein and he conveyed to me his concern about the way Ted's handling the defense."

"What are you saying? Elliot says he is doing a good job."

"Elliot is not a criminal lawyer; he is a doctor for God's sake. He doesn't know anything about this kind of matter. He found the wrong time to be stubborn. Hear me out, Ruth. I need you to listen to me and understand."

Ruth hated this type of manipulation. *'Listen well and understand,' means do what he wants me to do.* She kept silent, and let her father-in-law finish talking.

"Saul thinks that if the case continues the way it is going Elliot, God forbid, will lose. You know what that means? I am sure you would not like that."

"Why does Mr. Bernstein think…?"

"It's too complicated to go into. I don't understand all of it, but one thing Saul is saying is that bashing the police integrity is not working."

"Ted said the best defense is a good offense. He wants to put the police on trial…"

"But you can hear the experts on television saying the same thing as Saul. Definitely, it's wise to attack the evidence but not in every case is it intelligent to attack the police."

"Some say it might be a brilliant line of defense…"

"Some say… can you afford to take that chance? Well, I can't."

"What exactly do you want me to do?"

"I am glad you see the danger, Ruth. First you need to put some sense into Elliot's head. You need to persuade him that maybe Ted is not doing such a good job after all. Then, maybe he will listen to me and I can talk him into retaining Saul as his attorney."

"I don't know about that. I already tried to suggest... It will be hard to convince him... Ted is his best friend. I am afraid Elliot would be too about concerned about hurting Ted's feelings. Anyway, he believes Ted is doing a good job so far."

"Ruth, you are not listening. This is not a time to consider Ted's feelings. Elliot needs to understand that is a fight for his life."

"You're right Mr. Barrett. I'll try again to find a way to open up Elliot to that possibility. But in end, it will be his decision."

"I am planning to drive with Mrs. Barrett to New York and talk personally to Elliot. Call me right away after your conversation with him. This matter is urgent."

"Give my love to Mrs. Barrett."

"I will. And thanks, Ruth. Don't let me down. Don't let Elliot down."

Ruth hung up the phone and began pacing back and forth across the living room. The heavy wood smell of their recent remodeling still hung in the air. She took the small elevator to the fourth level of the guest quarters in anticipation of Elliot's parents' arrival. She inspected the floor and was pleased that the work was finished. She took the stairs to the children's floor and thought sadly of what they must be going through. She knew they stood behind their father but were greatly disturbed by the publicity. Her thought process worked better while she was busy, so she started dusting surfaces that already looked spotlessly clean.

The children's living quarters had been remodeled years ago to allow for two large bedrooms with plenty of storage space and private bathrooms. She passed through the rooms and trod the wood-railed stairs to the master bedroom. This floor and the first floor were remodeled when the children left home for college. The new paneling and the intricate molding were replaced to match the antique furniture. The huge main room took up half of the floor and the rest was designed to accommodate the marble bath and huge closets.

She moved swiftly, removing the almost invisible dust from the surface of the furniture. Then she went down to the main floor and stood in the dining room, staring emptily at the heavy table with twelve tall chairs.

Ruth's intuition had been trying to find expression since the end of the pretrial and was finally allowed to emerge. She had been feeling that there was something that did not make sense to her, but she could not put her finger on it. She also felt that the attack on the integrity of the police was not effective. She was always happy when Elliot opposed his father, but that this time she felt Mr. Barrett made good sense. He expressed what she herself had not been able to formulate. Ruth wanted to make sure that her basic dislike of Ted was not hindering her judgment. *Mr. Barrett is right. We cannot afford any chance that Elliot might be convicted. I must get more actively involved and not just trust Ted blindly.*

When Elliot came home from the clinic, Ruth conveyed her concern about Ted's line of defense. Elliot was very defensive and held firm in his belief that Ted was doing a good job.

"What if another lawyer outside of his firm can help Ted with his defense?" Ruth asked.

"Is my father putting ideas in your head?"

"No." Ruth hated to lie. "On other complicated court cases I've seen a few lawyers cooperating to…"

"This is not a complicated case. I am innocent and it will be easy to prove," Elliot responded angrily.

"No need to get angry. I'm just offering a suggestion," Ruth sounded defensive.

"I am sick and tired of everyone trying to suggest what I need to do," he shouted. *Does she suspect me?* he wondered.

"Everyone?" Ruth said, feeling hurt. "I am not everyone. I am your wife, for heaven's sake. I have stood by you from the first moment. And let me tell you something, it's not that easy. Elliot, what in the hell is going on with you?"

"You never really like Ted…"

"That is beside the point. Right now I'm thinking of what is good for you."

"How can you doubt Ted with all the time and effort he has been dedicating to me? He doesn't need that. He hasn't even discussed his fee with me."

Elliott left the room in a rage. He couldn't make himself apologize to Ruth, and felt he was sinking into a deep depression. The tension of sitting day after day in the courtroom and looking at photographs of Lindsey staring at him from the wall was upsetting. Now Ruth was challenging his judgment. It was too much to handle.

Ruth knew her anger made Elliot less open to her suggestions. She was worried about his loss of appetite and the deep sadness within his eyes. He stopped his regular visits to the gym with Ted. He retreated into long periods of silence and his vitality had almost vanished. Since the trial started, Elliot had shown barely any sexual interest in Ruth. The few times she managed to engage him in sex seemed almost without passion. *I must think of something I can do*, she concluded.

21

The next day in court, George started the final phase of his offense to establish intent and motive. He asked Assistant District Attorney Sharon Diller to conduct the direct examination. Sharon had a double major in law and psychology from Cornell University. At twenty-nine years old, with ample ambition, she had climbed fast to become George's number-one assistant. She was tall and skinny spoke in a high voice, and walked with a fast, vigorous pace. Thick glasses made her eyes look enlarged.

"State your name, please?" she asked her first witness.

"Dr. Larry Smith."

"Where do you practice medicine?"

"In New Jersey."

"Can you state your qualifications for the jury?"

Dr. Smith started to recount a long list of degrees and experience. Sharon wanted to impress the jury and Dr. Smith had impressive credentials. She had approached Dr. Smith, before Ted had the chance to recruit him to testify for the defense.

Sharon's brisk style of questioning led to a display of Dr. Smith's wide range of knowledge, about which he was delighted to boast. To Sharon's questions he provided a profile of a potential murder with motive and intent. In his estimation the murder occurred in a moment of rage between lovers: Afterwards, a careful, rational man consciously removed most of the physical evidence. In his estimation the person had something to hide—maybe an affair from his wife, or some other secret he did not want revealed. The crime scene did not point to a murderer who surprised the victim. She knew the assailant.

Ted made it clear in cross-examination of Dr. Smith that his theories were speculative, not to be viewed as factual. Under Sharon's redirect, Larry pointed to his record and insisted his observations came from his many years of experience in crime analysis. Ted again used his tricks to undermine the expert's testimony.

"Doctor, can you tell the jury how much money was given to you for testifying in this court case?"

"I earn my fees honestly," Larry said, experienced with that kind of probing.

"I charge for my time plus expenses."

"How many trials have you testified at in the past, and earned your fee honestly?" Ted asked sarcastically.

"Oh, I can't really remember right now, quite a few, I suppose."

Ted had done his homework. "Would you say exactly twenty-eight trials is an accurate number?" Ted continued.

"I suppose that is close…"

"I don't mean to cut you off, but can you tell us what you charge for your courtroom services?"

Smith knew when to retreat and still keep his dignity. "I charge a fair fee of two hundred dollars per hour for my courtroom time. For my research and written opinion, I charge one hundred and seventy-five dollars an hour. I guess it's much less than a trial lawyer would charge for his time," Smith replied with sarcasm.

"Your Honor, the witness is…" Ted complained.

"Strike the last remark from the record. Doctor, please refrain from personal comments," Judge Boyd directed.

Dr. Smith had spent many hours on the witness stand. He expected and enjoyed this kind of exchange. His eloquence when sitting on the witness stand empowered him. He had the capability to provoke or to help, as it suited him. This stellar reputation contributed to his being invited to be an expert witness at many trials. Mostly, he liked to detach himself from the drama in the courtroom and observe its participants. Most amusing to him was Judge Boyd, who could almost pass as one of his clinical patients. Judge Boyd seemed at times as if she were not in the courtroom. She would go into a dreamlike trance and be jolted awake when an objection was called. She snapped out of her thoughts and frowned, as if asking. 'How dare anyone disturb my reverie?' On other occasions she would stare with hawk-like eyes, moving her head back and forth listening intently to the dialogue as if her life depended on each word being said. She ruled with complete authority and control. Everyone, including the court clerk and stenographer, fell under her sway and seemed to want her approval, like children with their parents.

Dr. Smith was interested in Elliot, who claimed to be innocent while his whole demeanor said otherwise. His melancholy showed, despite his desperate attempt to create a rehearsed image, probably as his lawyer advised. When the victim's name came up, his nervous, unconscious body language and hardened facial muscles pointed to a hidden agenda. Dr. Smith felt compassion for Ruth, who found herself in a place where she did not belong, yet sent loving supportive looks across the room to Elliot throughout the day.

Ted was a whole other subject of study. His wardrobe suggested a social climbing personality that had risen high, and he liked it up there. He would try winning this case at any price. His desire to win also revealed an almost hidden motive, shown at times by thinly disguised confusion. Sometimes, during an emotional delivery, he would make a Freudian slip.

George seemed fit to be a judge instead of the ruthless prosecutor he was not.

And Smith himself, well, that was another story. He was elated in his superior role of being able to watch everyone and tell everyone how good and knowledgeable he was. He enjoyed seeing the jury's admiring eyes watching him with respect.

George rested his case, feeling that his team had delivered a good, convincing presentation. Now, the defendant's team was ready to present their witnesses. He was curious to hear Margaret's testimony. He knew it could hurt his case, but was not overly worried. His final argument would be strong.

Ted was eager to start his defense. He stood up and with a facial expression that expressed confidence announced, "I call Ms. Margaret Anderson to the witness stand."

You could hear a pin drop as Margaret walked slowly to the witness stand.

All eyes followed her intently, a woman who had lost her only child. She was sworn in and sat teary-eyed in the witness seat. Margaret could only comprehend the last part of the sworn statement. "…the truth and only the truth so help you God."

"I do," she said, thinking: *I truly need God's help.*

To impress the jury, Ted planned to start with her emotional testimony. He needed the strong testimony Margaret would deliver, to sway the jury away from the effect of the strong physical evidence and the testimony the psychologist had just presented. Ted appreciated the excellent job George was doing. Now, he had a chance to meet the challenge. He was grateful Margaret still held her strong belief that Elliot was not involved in her daughter's death. He brushed away disturbing thoughts of guilt he might feel at causing Margaret additional grief. He knew he must remain focused and take advantage of this important witness.

"We all know how hard it is for you today," Ted said in soft a voice. "We're sorry you have had to suffer so much. We have a few questions for you today, if it's all right. If you want me to pause at any point, please let me know." Then, with an even softer voice, he continued. "Were you the first person to find Lindsey?"

"Yes I was," Margaret said quietly.

"Please tell the jury in your own words, why you went to Lindsey's house that evening."

"Yes. I live in New Jersey. Since my successful operation, done by Dr. Barrett, I go to the hospital for chemotherapy and checkups." She looked at Elliot, and by nodding her head, said hello to him. Elliot nodded back. "That night I came to my daughter's house because, it's easier to take the subway to the hospital in the morning. I didn't call to let her know. I knew it would be all right."

"So you were the one who found her two days after her tragic death?"

"Yes."

"Tell us in your own words what happened."

"I have my own key, because I never know when my daughter is home. I opened the door to the gallery and went upstairs to her apartment." Margaret began sobbing.

Ted offered her a Kleenex. Ted didn't want her to stop but said, "Take as much time as you need."

"I'm all right." She continued, taking a deep breath. "Lindsey was laying on the sofa and I knew something was wrong. I went to check her body. It was cold without life... She was dead... It was awful ..." Margaret's was sobbing loudly.

Ted waited until Margaret had calmed down. "When you saw her, how was she lying? Did you move her to learn if she were alive?" Ted had been waiting a long time to ask that question.

"Objection, he is leading the witness," George said.

"Sustained."

"How did you find out your daughter was dead?"

"I was in shock...I don't quite remember what I did. I know I checked her face to see if she were alive. When the police asked if I moved anything, I think I told them I didn't. But now I don't quite remember. It seems so far away."

Ted was pleased by her confusion. It opened the possibility for him to bring his theoretical questions to the forefront in his rebuttal. "We will get back to this later. On another subject, I want to ask if your daughter asked you to bring all your medicine for Dr. Barrett's inspection."

"Yes. My daughter told me that Dr. Barrett wanted to see all the medication I was taking. I'm glad he was going to this for me. I was prescribed medicines by different doctors and the combination of drugs was not good for me. I thank Dr. Barrett for changing my medicine. It really made a difference." She looked at Elliot with a small smile.

"Did Dr. Barrett come to visit you at Lindsey's apartment?"

"Yes. Before and after the operation, when I stayed with my daughter. She took such good care of me. He came several times."

George was busy taking notes for his cross. He knew that Margaret was a very good witness for Ted. Who could be better than the mother of the deceased providing supporting testimony for the defendant? He would be sure to be sensitive and not take advantage of Margaret's grief and confusion and yet make her seem not reliable. Jurors did not appreciate when either attorney attacked a witness without sufficient reason. Sometimes, it was better to retreat, and let the defense score a few points just to make it seem as if it was fair game instead of winning at all costs. George decided to ask Margaret to remember more precisely the number of calls she had received from Elliot, and exactly how many times Elliot visited the apartment while she was there. He was curious to know if she knew about any visits made without her being present.

Ted continued his direct, getting all the emotional drama he needed with his questions about Lindsey, her tragic abandonment by the father she loved and her own life without marriage. Ted was so focused on eliciting the testimony that he forgot he actually knew all the details. Listening intently to Margaret, he led the jurors through an emotional journey that transfixed them. Ted stretched out his questions out until the end of the day in order to leave the jury with Lindsey's mother emotional and effective testimony.

22

George was hoping to counter the strong effect of Margaret's testimony and tried to hide his disappointment. He could not show any antagonism toward Margaret because of the sympathy she had received the day before. Nevertheless, he had to clear up the picture for the jury. He approached the witness stand and explained that she could stop her testimony at any time if it might become too much for her to speak. A box of tissue was in easy reach. He expressed his appreciation for the difficulty of the questions, but stressed that they were necessary in order to determine Lindsey's killer.

"You gave a statement to the police that you hadn't touched anything the night you found Lindsey's body?"

"Yes sir."

"Then you said the same thing to Detective Benjamin Sills when he questioned you. Then in the preliminary hearing you testified under oath that you thought Lindsey's face was turned upward when you entered the apartment the first time. What is your testimony today?" George was firm but cordial.

"I don't quite remember…"

"Would you say your memory was better then, as things happened, than right now?" George used an old trick.

"I suppose so." Margaret seemed confused.

"Then, would you agree that your testimony then was more accurate?"

"Objection." Ted knew it was a valid line of questioning. He himself used it with witnesses, but he wanted to cut the flow of

George's questions, to reduce their impact and relieve Margaret's pressure.

"Overruled," said Judge Boyd. Looking at Ted she seemed to imply, 'Stop trying that kind of tactic with me.'

"What made you change your testimony?" George pressed on.

Ted was afraid George would ask that question. "Well, when Ted asked me about this, I didn't remember. What's the difference? I found her dead." Margaret was disturbed.

George jumped at the opportunity as if he had found gold. "It is very important for the sake of truth, Mrs. Anderson. Please, when did the defense attorney ask you this question?"

"It was right after the preliminary hearing testimony."

Ted sank into his chair, feeling sweat form on his forehead.

"Your Honor, I need to discuss this matter with you. May we approach the bench?" George asked urgently.

After Judge Boyd halted the proceedings and excused the jury, she demanded to know what was happening.

"Your Honor, there is nothing in the discovery about this interview," George said.

Judge Boyd looked angrily at Ted, demanding an answer.

"It was something I forgot about," Ted pretended with an innocent voice.

"This does not happen in my courtroom." Judge Boyd was furious.

"It wasn't really an interview. I asked her two questions in the hallway, and I completely forgot about it afterward."

The judge was not pleased with Ted's excuses. "I fine you one thousand dollars. The next time something like that happens I am going to hold you in contempt of court, and the consequences will be more severe."

"I am truly sorry. It will never happen again," Ted apologized.

George wanted to seize the opportunity. Margaret's testimony was going too well for Ted. "Your honor, I call for a motion to strike all of Mrs. Anderson's testimony from the record."

"I instructed the jury to strike the questions regarding the issue of Margaret's confusion." Judge Boyd agreed.

George hoped the motion damaged the defense's case. The judge's ruling in his favor put a major dent in Ted's line of questioning.

The jury was called back. They seemed curious about what had happened in their absence. Several times a day after being excused, the jurors left the courtroom. Some of them took the opportunity to stretch their legs after so many hours of sitting and listening to endless, and at times tedious, questions and answers.

Judge Boyd explained the technicality of the problem and asked them to disregard all questions and answers that pertained to the position of the victim's head.

Ted had suffered a setback, but he knew some effect would remain despite the judge's directive. He had managed to instill doubt about the prosecution's case.

George, encouraged, continued his cross. "How many telephone calls did you place from your daughter's telephone to Dr. Barrett in the last six months?"

"Oh, I can't recall something like that." Margaret sounded surprised by the question.

"I don't mean exactly, just approximately."

"I really can't remember…"

"Okay, would you say fifty calls?"

"No. Not that many."

"Would you say thirty?"

"No. I don't believe that many either."

"Would you say between twenty to thirty?"

"Objection. The witness said she doesn't remember." Ted tried to save the moment.

"Try to answer the question, Mrs. Anderson," Judge Boyd ruled.

"Maybe close to ten."

George was pleased. "No more questions."

At the end of each day, Judge Boyd warned the jurors to refrain from drawing any conclusions until the end of final arguments. She reminded them not to discuss the case, even amongst themselves.

"We will adjourn until tomorrow morning at 9 A.M." she announced, in a monotonous tone that agitated particularly Elliot.

That is a great idea. Please jury, do not form any conclusions, Ted wished bitterly. Ted had almost succeeded in putting a serious dent in the prosecution's theory, but found himself on the downside. He was succeeding until George revealed his failure to deliver a crucial piece of discovery. *Not all is lost*, Ted thought, *although the emotional testimony drained me.*

Ruth felt agitated. Things were not going well. She expected that the state would present a strong argument, but counted on Ted to come up with a definite argument that would show Elliot's innocence. She had been swayed by Ted's optimism, and his promise that when he started his direct everything would be clear. The first witness for the defense was meant to provide powerful evidence, but this had happened.

"Ted, what is going on?" Ruth asked. "You said that in the prosecutor's phase they would look good. Now it's your phase and it's still not going well."

Ted was fatigued. The last thing he wanted to do was to give more explanations. "As I said before, it's the nature of the courtroom. One day you're up and the next day you're down. Don't jump to any conclusions after one day."

"We are counting on you," Ruth said.

"I know. I am doing more than my best. This is only the beginning."

"Ruth is overly worried," Elliot said to Ted. He looked at Ruth and said, "Ted knows what he is doing."

"Thanks for the confidence," Ted said. "Everything will be all right. Let's all get some rest. I'll see you tomorrow in the courtroom."

On the drive home, Ruth was agitated. Elliot's words echoed

in her mind. '*Ruth is overly worried.' How dare he? He's the one that shows all the signs of being overly worried, but he tries to project his feelings onto me.* She observed Elliot who was looking out the car window with an ambivalent expression. Again she wondered. *Margaret's testimony revealed Elliot's involvement with that family was more than just a normal doctor-patient relationship. Was he hiding something?*

She had promised not to bring up the issue again, but wondered if she should break that promise. What was the best thing to do? They arrived at Elliot's clinic. He liked to spend time at his clinic each day after court had adjourned. "It helps keep my sanity," he explained. She decided she would talk to him later that evening.

The telephone was ringing as she entered her home. She hurried to pick up the receiver.

"Ruth?"

"How are you, Mr. Barrett?"

"Is Elliott there?"

"No, he's at the clinic."

"Good. Actually I am not fine at all. As a matter of fact, I am truly disturbed about what happened in the courtroom today."

"You already know about the testimony today?" Ruth was surprised.

"It's all over the television. I also heard from my connection. We must do something, and very soon. I thought you would get back to me sooner."

"I tried to speak to Elliot but he got angry, and refused to talk about it."

"You must do better than that, Ruth. You must pound some sense into his brain.

This family is going down the drain."

"I agree. I'm frustrated myself. I'm going to force the issue tonight when he comes home from the clinic."

"Do that. I'm also going to talk with him. Keep me posted. "

"I will," Ruth said. She meant it.

Elliot returned home from the clinic later than usual. Ruth saw he was depressed and reluctantly decided she would find another time to talk to him. She knew he would not be receptive to her questions. Could he handle any more stress? She wondered what was going on in his mind. Day after day she observed him sitting in the courtroom, not saying much at the end of the session. She tried speaking to him, to cheer him up with her forced optimistic outlook, but Elliot seemed withdrawn in to his own world and gave the impression that he did not want to be disturbed. Even Ted stopped instructing him to show a more cheerful face. Ruth hoped everything would return to normal once Elliot was acquitted.

23

Ruth felt almost incapacitated. Her frustrations grew. She didn't know what to do, but she knew she had to do something. Letting intuition guide her action, she wanted to see where Lindsey had lived.

One afternoon, she left Elliot a note saying she had gone shopping and would be home later. A taxi took her downtown to Prince Street and she got out in front of Lindsey's gallery. Ruth felt maybe there was something in this place that might reveal the truth of what happened on the night of September the twenty-eighth. She walked through the thriving commercial, residential and artistic streets, observing the great details of the architectural ornamentation. The exquisite cast-iron buildings and cobblestone facades were painted in a variety of attractive colors.

It was a late gray afternoon, and the streetlights had been turned on. The art galleries were open, filled with of browsers. Ruth recognized Lindsey's building from photographs shown in the courtroom. A woman had been murdered here and Elliot was wrongfully accused of the crime.

The sign bore the name NIRVANA GALLERY with the Far East style and coloring. The massive front window was visible in remnants of yellow police tape that not long ago had cordoned off the crime scene. There was something very pleasant about the proportion and placement of the facade design. The abstract testimony from the trial became alive as she stood in front of the actual building where the tragic events had taken place. *What in heaven's sake am I doing here? What do I think I can find here?* She thought, and almost decided to leave immediately—but was compelled to stay a little longer.

The sound of a bell from a nearby church tolling the eight o'clock hour jolted her. The darkness brought on illuminating streetlights. Ruth walked down Prince Street aimlessly and encountered a group of people watching a young man kneeling down over a spray-painted canvas. She was fascinated with his paintings. They looked like a universe of imaginary worlds, yet seemed somehow realistic. The artist briskly and proficiently changed the spray can colors as he painted. He used the simplest tools to form the shapes he needed. Using his bare hands, he covered the areas he wanted to shield from the spray. He seemed oblivious to his observers and kept his movements swift, only stopping to make fast observation of his work and then, with enthusiasm, return to his painting.

Ruth liked the blue, purple and turquoise painting and impulsively wanted to purchase it. She moved closer to the painter and noticed his wide, innocent blue eyes. He had an untamed beard and wore a big black leather hat. His body was boyishly frail, which made his overalls look a few sizes too big.

"How much is this painting?" Ruth pointed at the painting she liked. It had spirals floating on a background of space that gave her a feeling deep inside herself.

The young man stopped working and looked at Ruth as if asking 'Do I want to sell it to you?' He wiped his stained hands on his multicolored pants legs and picked up the painting.

"How much are you willing to pay?" he asked with an amiable smile.

"I don't know… What do you usually ask for this…?"

"What if I say one hundred bucks?"

"Well, then it's a hundred dollars. I am willing to support a young artist." She searched her purse to find her wallet.

"Are you buying it because you like it or because you feel you need to support me?" he said as if insulted.

"Oh no, I love it. I really do." Ruth said apologetically.

"No apology needed. Now that you like it, the actual price is forty-five bucks," he said, laughing with the crowd of onlookers, amused by the exchange.

"What if I gave you a hundred?" Ruth was impressed with his honesty.

"Then I would accept the hundred."

"What is your name, young man?" she asked as she handed him the money.

"Stevie, what's yours?"

He wrapped the painting with a sheet of newspaper and handed it to her.

"My name is Ruth. Where did you learn how to paint so beautifully?"

"By myself, no one taught me."

"Where do you live?"

"Right now I live in the street. Right around there." He pointed to a space between two buildings.

"In the street? What do you mean? You are too young and talented to live in the street. Where are your parents?"

"Oh, that's a long story." He shrugged.

Ruth was on the board of a charity that found solutions for homeless people. Ruth felt compassion for this young man who, like thousands of homeless people, was wasting his life on the streets.

"Stevie, can I take you out for dinner?"

"Do you ask because you feel sorry for me?"

"Nonsense. I am just interested in your life. Isn't that a good enough reason?"

"I already made my sale of the day. And yours is a good enough reason. Besides, I am hungry so maybe everybody will be happy." His ironic smile remained throughout their conversation.

Ruth's telephone rang from inside her purse. "One of those rich ladies," Stevie thought, as he started packing his equipment into a cardboard box.

"Ruth, where are you?" Elliot sounded worried.

"I left you a note saying I was shopping."

"I didn't see the note… just a minute… I see it now. But where are you?"

"I'm shopping. I'll be back in a few hours."

"Please don't be too late."

"Dinner is ready, just warm it up. Love you." Ruth put the phone back in her purse, pleased that Elliot missed her.

"Where can we eat around here?" Ruth asked.

"Even with my work clothes, I know we can get served at the deli around the corner."

During the meal, Ruth learned that Stevie was a brilliant, twenty-three-year old young man. His parents had traveled in a bus all over America as hippies in the '60s.

They had Stevie late in life and gave up their nomadic ways for a yuppie lifestyle in Connecticut. They now owned a beautiful house in suburban Hartford. Growing up hearing them talking about the sixties, Stevie felt that they had sold out; in protest, he moved out of the house when he was 16. Since then he had been living on the streets of Manhattan.

He kept in touch with his parents by calling them periodically and making rare visits home. He told Ruth that he always had enough money for food and, most importantly, for his painting supplies.

"That's no way to live," Ruth exclaimed. "I can find you a nice place."

Stevie seemed amused. "I left the quote 'nice place to live' a long time ago. I'm happy and free to do what I want. The only thing important in life is freedom, not what society has to offer."

"Oh, don't be so idealistically naïve. There are other things life can offer."

"Like what? What is more important?" Stevie challenged her.

"Family, companionship, some comfort, money to do what you want. What about a place to stay, what's wrong with that?" Ruth was trying to persuade Stevie to accept a permanent home she could provide through her charity.

"I have a place to stay. Companionship? I meet people all day long. The question is what price do I have to pay to get more comfort?"

"You need to work just like everyone else does and you do work. You just need to work for more money."

"Work? That's too high a price for me to pay; I can't compromise my freedom. My painting is my work. What's wrong with that?" Stevie smiled, as if saying he couldn't be beat at this game.

"Of course you should paint. You're a good artist—but what I mean is work in a better environment. The spray paint you are breathing is very toxic. There are ways you can protect yourself."

Stevie decided to change the subject, feeling uncomfortable with the intrusion, but Ruth wasn't deterred.

"Listen Stevie, I need to get back home, but I really want to talk to you again. Let me see where you're staying."

"Oh, that's not necessary," Stevie laughed. "I'm a big boy."

"I know. I didn't mean it that way. I was just curious."

"OK. Just don't tell me you are shocked when we get there."

They walked past Lindsey's building, and around the corner they entered an alley space located between two buildings. The rough alley walls were tall without windows. Ruth felt wary in the dark space and was careful not to step on anything or slip on an unseen object. At the end of the alley, beyond a garbage container, Stevie had built a cardboard structure with a mattress inside it. "You see, I told you I have a place to stay. This is my chateau. It's all I need."

Ruth was appalled. The smell from the nearby garbage container was nauseating. "Chateau? You are really a funny guy. What about this garbage…?"

"This container protects me from the blowing wind. The smell? Smells are part of life. Do you know smell is the strongest of our senses?"

That was too much for Ruth even to try to argue. She wanted

to get out of there as fast as possible. "Well, I can't stand a smell like that," she said as she started to walk back to the lighted street. Stevie roared with laughter. "I told you, you would…"

"You win again," she said, trying to hold back her breath.

She was glad to be back on the well-lit street. It seemed as if she re-entered the world from the other side of darkness. Stevie walked beside her, as if seeing her to the door. "So, is it all right to meet again?" Ruth asked.

"Hey, if you pay for the food and promise not to try to find me a better place to live, it's a deal."

24

In an early meeting in the District Attorney's office George asked his deputies to comment on the probable outcome of the trial. A few placed their chance of success at sixty-five percent or so, not a particularly favorable percentage. He decided to approach Ted one more time with his earlier offer of a plea bargain.

"I have a final proposition for you." George said to Ted. "It may be my last offer. I have a pile of cases waiting for me. My previous offer for a plea bargain still stands. What do you say we close on a deal?"

Ted knew where this offer was coming from. "I have no authority to give you an answer," Ted replied, "but I think I can assure you that Dr. Barrett will not plea bargain. He won't admit any implication of murder. He made that clear to me."

"Don't say later that I was not a fair man. Truthfully, the way I assess how things are going, we are pretty even, but you know how juries are. They are unpredictable."

Ted conveyed the offer to Elliot and Ruth before court reconvened. He hoped Elliot would accept the plea bargain; he wanted the whole nightmare to be over. After he explained all the ramifications of George's offer, Elliot rejected it completely. "I am innocent all the way to the end," he insisted.

"Do you feel we are at risk, Ted? Do you think we should consider the plea?"

Ruth asked.

"Not at all… I simply must convey George's offer to you. It's my duty as your lawyer.

I'm still certain we will win," Ted said, not really totally believing it at all.

Ruth felt uneasiness in her stomach. She sensed that Ted was not being completely honest. His demeanor and his avoidance of eye contact convinced her she must take more control of the situation. "Why are you so sure?" she asked. "To tell you the truth, there are days when I do not share your confidence. From what I understand from listening to the television commentators, this case can go either way."

Ted felt even more uncomfortable. "Television commentators are there to create sensationalism. I don't listen to them. All my energy is on this case. I don't share your pessimism. I think we are doing just fine."

Elliot was going crazy. "Ruth, you must have patience."

"I'm not a pessimist," Ruth protested, "I'm a realist and I just wonder if there is anything else that can be done." She had not told Elliot about his father's wishes, but they were uppermost in her mind.

"We are almost at the end of the trial. The truth will come out. Leave it at that," Elliot said, pulling lightly at Ruth's arm, signaling for her to stop the conversation.

In court, Ted continued with his direct. He wanted to show the gentle aspects of Elliot's character and to emphasize he was a caring doctor. The witnesses he called to the stand established that Elliot was a dedicated, highly qualified professional. They testified that he had a holistic approach to healing that included proper nutrition, stress management, psychological as well as physiological care. They stressed his good reputation and his expertise in the operating room. The intention was to present Elliot as an upstanding man, a respectable physician, not a person who could commit murder.

In his cross, George accepted the image that Ted had presented. Undoubtedly, Elliot was a good man and had an impeccable reputation. George made it clear he was not interested in attacking his character or questioning the doctor's credentials. He used Ted's presentation to argue that Elliot had a lot to lose if his affair with Lindsey was discovered.

At one point George looked directly at Elliot and said, "I challenge the defendant to come forth as a witness and stand before the jury for questioning." That request created a disturbance in the courtroom, and a harsh response from Judge Boyd. She would not tolerate excessive theatrics.

Ted's next witness was Dr. Berry Rosenthal, an expert in marital and family counseling. He testified that Elliot was the antitheses of a man who would have an extra-marital affair. He explained, in a pleasant baritone voice, that he had interviewed Elliot and found him to be a rational man with a healthy relationship with his wife and his children. They had no history of violence or any need to consult a family therapist. Their marriage and their children's stability and success showed a stable, supportive, and loving family. He went on to dispute with irony any character speculation as without scientific merit. "A man like Dr. Barrett is unlikely to consider engaging in an affair."

Dr. Rosenthal's smug testimony angered George, and he quickly rose to challenge his credentials. "Mr. Rosenthal," George said, omitting the title *doctor* on purpose.

"Are you a psychiatrist?"

"No, I'm a family therapist."

"So you are not really a doctor, a physician?"

"I have a doctorate."

"Not from a medical school. But never mind. You seem to give all kinds of opinions from a range of areas of expertise."

"I have given my opinion as was asked to do, and as I know from my study and field experience based on thirty-five years of practice and also from my interview with the defendant." Dr. Rosenthal's response was confident and quick.

"I know you have an airplane to catch, but can you speak a

little slower? It's hard for the stenographer to record what is being said." George wanted to get him annoyed but could not succeed.

"I have no airplane to catch; I have all the time needed to answer any questions…"

"I didn't mean to cut you off," George moved in for an old trick to discredit the witness. "Can you tell the jury how much money you are making in this court case?"

"Nothing. I'm not accepting a fee for my testimony."

"Nothing? And why not?" George asked incredulously. He immediately realized he had made a big mistake. He had fallen into the trap he had tried to set. He had learned as a student not to ask questions in court when he didn't already know the answer.

"I am here for justice. A fellow doctor is in trouble. I am here to tell the truth and set the record straight."

Ted had hoped George would ask that question. Dr. Rosenthal's response put George in an embarrassing position that ridiculed him in the eyes of the jury. The ironic smiles from some jury members did not escape his notice. Ted managed to steal a glance at George's fallen face and pointed to George as if saying, 'I scored another point.' He didn't get any response.

Media commentators directed attention to George's mistake. They also made much of George's dramatic move to challenge Elliot to come to the witness stand and testify. It was becoming a central issue with the media. Would he testify? The reporters bombarded Elliot with that question each time they saw him.

"If Dr. Barrett is not guilty, why wouldn't he stand before the jury and convince them of his innocence?" one reporter asked Ted. Ted responded elegantly that it had not been ruled out as a possibility and would be decided when appropriate.

At the end of another tiring day in court, Ruth and Elliot returned home. They were silently eating dinner when the doorbell rang. Ruth opened the door and, to her astonishment, there stood Mr. and Mrs. Barrett.

"Come in," Ruth said. "Come and join us in the dining room."

Elliot came to see who was at the door. "Why didn't you all first?" He asked, clearly annoyed.

"We didn't want you to tell us not to come," Mr. Barrett responded. "We came to talk with you."

At the dinner table, Mr. Barrett immediately began to stress his point that his lawyer in Boston thought Ted was not doing a sufficient job. He added his own opinion that there was an urgent need to explore other options.

"You're not telling me anything you didn't mention on the phone. I have all the trust in the world in Ted," Elliot said, red-faced with anger. "You always think you know everything. How do you know how Ted is performing, from watching television?" Elliot shouted this last challenge to his father.

Ruth, knowing what was going to happen, tried to stop Mr. Barrett from answering but Mr. Barrett shouted back: "We know everything from our own man sitting in the court..." He realized that in the heat of the moment he said what he hadn't meant to say.

Elliot jumped up from his seat. "Are you spying on me?"

"You are refusing to cooperate and you leave me no choice."

Elliot turned toward Ruth. "Did you know about this?"

"This is between you and your parents. Leave me out of it."

"Your name and reputation are not all that is under attack. What about the shame we have to endure?" Mrs. Barrett said, supporting her husband. "You don't know how much we have suffered."

"Right now that's the last thing on my mind," Elliot said, his voice rising.

Ruth had never seen Elliot's family in engage in such a heated argument and desperately tried to calm them down. The television screen in the kitchen which was turned, on switched to covering Elliot's trial and they all went there to watch the news. They listened to the commentary about George's brilliant job in the courtroom, and the commentator's opinion that Ted was desperately trying to argue a difficult case.

The yelling resumed immediately after the coverage ended. "You see. You didn't want to listen to good advice!" Mr. Barrett shouted. "I know for certain, my lawyer would have known how to handle this case much better."

Elliot rose from the table and left the room, slamming the door behind him. The surprise and shock hushed everyone else.

"Elliot is under tremendous stress," Ruth said quietly. "Please, let's all calm down."

Mr. Barrett signaled to Mrs. Barrett that it was time to go.

"We're staying at the Plaza Hotel. Tomorrow morning we'll all be in the courtroom, and we plan to stay until the end of the trial."

"You can stay here," Ruth said. "Please, there's plenty of room. You can have plenty of privacy."

"We think it's better this way," Mr. Barrett said tersely.

Mr. Barrett called for a taxi. Ruth was distressed, but relieved. *There was too much tension already. Their presence, no matter how well intended, would only add more discomfort to her home.*

25

The silence that Elliot's parents left behind was as weary to Ruth's ears as the loudness and chaos had been. She sat for a long time at the kitchen table, trying to understand the explosion and Elliot's sudden departure. He was probably fuming upstairs. She had never seen Mr. Barrett express anger toward Elliot. She felt bad that she had not been truthful with Elliot about Mr. Barrett's representative in the courtroom and knew he was angry with her. Reluctantly, she started to load dishes into the dishwasher, throwing away the uneaten food still left on the plates. Tears rolled down her cheeks. She felt the continued pain of the extreme turn of events that had invaded her life.

When Ruth went upstairs to check on Elliot, she saw he was asleep. She noticed that it was past 8:30 and remembered that she had planned to go see Stevie. Earlier that day she had found a solution for Steve's situation—a grant that would pay for tuition at an experimental art school, and a cheap loft. She left a note for Elliot in case he woke up She to telling Stevie about the good news. It would be better than another night of silence at home with Elliot.

Stevie's face lit up when Ruth arrived. He was still on the street, trying to sell his painting. "You really came back to see me," Stevie said, surprised.

"I told you I would."

"Many people say all kinds of things, but never do anything about it."

"What about sharing another meal together?"

"I thought you would never ask," he said gladly. "I forgot to eat dinner."

"By the way, where do you take a shower?" Ruth asked. She was warming him up to accept her proposal. Stevie laughed at her bluntness. "I use a hose."

"What about in the winter?"

"What about it? You mean when it's cold?" He unleashed his special roaring laugh. "You are too civilized. Coldness is relative. When you get used to too much comfort you are too affected by the weather."

"You have an answer for everything, don't you?" Ruth said, still horrified by Stevie's despicable situation.

"The mind is the most important thing we have. You civilized…"

"Yeah, yeah, yeah, we civilized have a proposition for you free nomad."

"Not again!"

"Let's go," she said with a forgiving gesture. They walked to the deli and sat in a corner booth. The waitress recognized Stevie and seemed puzzled by his appearance with the well-groomed woman. The waitress and Stevie exchanged a short conversation and she tried to question him, with her eyes, about Ruth's identity. "This is Ruth, my new friend," he said proudly.

"Nice meeting you. I'm Jody." Ruth only ordered coffee but encouraged Stevie to order a full meal. He ordered a hamburger, French fries and a coke. Ruth decided not to comment on his choices. Maybe vegetables were civilized for him. She didn't want to be sound too parental. She knew it was important to find a path to his heart. Jody took their order to the chef.

"Girl?" Ruth asked.

"Just another babe I know." He smiled.

"Seriously Stevie, I want to talk to you. I think you have real talent. I found a way for you to expand your creativity and not compromise your freedom."

"What is it to you?" Stevie asked suspiciously.

"When I was young, I used to live on a big ranch in Texas. After I left, I almost forgot what freedom meant. You made me remember. I recapture that sense of freedom when I'm outdoors in nature or riding my horse in the hills. Then I feel the whole world belongs to me."

"Hey, you're cool. But did you also sell out like my parents?"

"No… well, I moved to New York, got married, raised children, just got busy with what I needed to do…" Ruth looked up at the ceiling as if trying to recapture that time in her life when she had no worries. Now there was only confusion.

"Anyway," she said, returning from her daydream, "What were you saying?"

The food arrived and Stevie and Jody exchanged flirting glances. Ruth watched how Stevie ate with pleasure. He seemed fragile and almost childlike, yet resilient and tough from years of living on the street.

"Let's hear your great solution for me," he said with his ironic smile.

"I'm on the board of a group that helps individuals solve certain kinds of problems." She was careful to avoid using the word 'homeless'. "You can get a place to live and also have a workshop where you can express your individuality without any 'civilized' influence. All for free."

"I don't know… Leave my chateau?"

"Chateau," she laughed. "You mean the dump? I am proposing a place with a shower, a clean, safe bed and a heater for the cold winter."

"Clean, safe, warm, civilized comforts that spoil the raw senses."

"OK, no one says you have to turn on the heater if you don't want to…" Ruth noticed Stevie's attention was drawn to the television set above the counter. She saw herself, Elliot, and Ted leaving the courtroom as reporters bombarded them with questions.

"Hey, Ruth, you're on the television and...and wait a minute, I know that dude!" Stevie shouted with excitement.

"It's me and my husband...but how do you know my husband?"

"That's your husband?" Stevie sounded shocked. "I saw him the day of the murder on Prince Street. He parked his car in my alley."

Ruth's face grew pale. She thought she might faint. "Are you sure you saw him?" Ruth had suspicions that Elliot was hiding something but this was confirmation. *Stevie saw Elliot the day of the murder.* Horrified thoughts flashed through her mind.

"Yes, just like I am seeing you. With his fancy suit and fancy car." Ruth's mind raced. Mr. Blumenthal had testified that the car was parked on the street next to his store, not in an alley. "Are you sure he parked his car in your alley?" Ruth asked.

"Of course. It's not everyday someone parks a red Jaguar at my place."

"Red Jaguar?" Ruth was completely confused. "Not a Mercedes?"

"Hey, I'm not that far from civilization. I know the difference between a Jaguar and a Mercedes."

"Okay... Wait a minute." It hit her like a flash of lightning. "Which man are you talking about?" Ruth pointed to the television.

"That dude, on the left of you. The one with the fancy suit."

"You mean Ted?"

"I don't know his name. Ruth, what's happening to you? You're as white as a ghost."

"Are you certain? Please tell me one more time..."

"Ruth, I'm telling you."

"Listen Stevie, I have to go."

"What's going on?" Stevie asked, confused.

"Here is my card with my phone number. Think about my proposal. Don't just reject it. I'll see you soon."

"Tell me what is going on."

"Here's money to pay for the food. I have to go. I'll explain to you another time."

Ruth left Stevie bewildered, hailed a taxi and asked the driver to rush to her home. She could not wait to get home and tell Elliot what she had just discovered. Her mind was racing with questions, trying to comprehend what her discovery would mean. She was sorry to leave in such a rush. She wanted to ask Stevie more questions.

How to explain being there that night? What brought him there? Was he involved in Lindsey's murder? He must be. It's really more reasonable for Ted to be the one to have an affair, not Elliot. He fits the police profile perfectly. What if Stevie is mistaken? But he can't be. He says he can identify him with certainty. But is Stevie reliable? Yes, he saw Ted's red Jaguar that night in the alley. Stevie was absolutely certain about it. How could he have known Ted had a red Jaguar? It must be Ted's car. I need to go to the police right away. But what do I say to the police? They won't believe me. They'll think I'm crazy.

Ruth's confusion played back and forth in her mind as euphoria and doubt surfaced with equal intensity. She began reconsidering pest events and odd pieces of conversation. She remembered Heather saying at Thanksgiving before the date of Lindsey's murder that she and Ted were considering divorce.

Now I understand, Ruth thought bitterly. *I know why Ted suddenly shifted his behavior. He didn't want to attract any attention to himself. Now I understand my discomfort about him all along, especially when we lost the preliminary hearing.*

"The son of a bitch," she suddenly said out loud. She realized that Ted was trying to nail Elliot so he would not be caught. *The police were completely blind.* Ruth's anger boiled over. She could not wait to get home to tell Elliot what she had discovered. Soon their world would be right again.

26

When the taxi arrived at Ruth's residence, she gave the driver a large bill and didn't wait for change. She opened the front door and ran upstairs to the bedroom where Elliot was still deep in sleep.

"Elliot. Elliot. Wake up. Wake up!" Ruth shook him with excitement.

"What's going on? What time is it?" Elliot had trouble waking up.

"Oh no, did you take sleeping pills again?"

"Had to. I needed to sleep."

"Well, you must wake up. I have something very important to tell you." Ruth was bursting with fervor.

"Can't it wait until the morning?" Elliot said drowsily, turning away to roll back into a sleeping position.

Ruth rushed to the bathroom and brought back a towel soaked with cold water. "Let me wipe your face. You must wake up." She managed to help him sit up and wake up just enough to pay attention to her. "Listen, you won't believe what I just found out tonight. Ted is the one who murdered Lindsey."

"Ted? Are you out of your mind? What…?"

"I knew you would say that," she snapped, "but listen, there is a man who saw

Ted parked his car by the gallery on the night of the murder."

Elliot sat up, now trying to fight the effect of the sleeping pills. "What in the hell are you talking about? What man?"

"Please. Just listen to me. I was sitting in a restaurant with Stevie…"

"Huh?"

"Can you just listen? He is a young artist and I'm trying to help him find a home. I was talking to him at a deli when the news on the television showed us leaving the courthouse with Ted. Stevie identified Ted as the one who parked his car next to Lindsey's building the night she was murdered."

"That just can't be… first of all… how he can be so certain and second …?"

"He saw Ted enter the alley, and he saw his red Jaguar! Hell, I didn't even say anything about the car … He, Stevie, said 'red Jaguar'… I am telling you Elliot, listen to me; it was Ted all along. He is trying to put the blame on you so he won't be caught."

Elliot rubbed his eyes in an attempt to become more alert. "That's insane. You're talking nonsense. Ted is my best friend. Why would he do something like that to me?"

"I was thinking about all this on the way home. It's all making sense now. He didn't try to frame you on purpose, but when you were arrested and you called him, he was trapped. Of course he couldn't tell you he did it. How could he? The profile from the police… doesn't it fit him …?"

"I just don't buy any of it." Elliot was fully awake now.

"Fine, then. I do," she said furiously. "I'm going to the police tomorrow morning, and I'll demand that they reopen the investigation."

"They'll laugh at you. Here is the wife of the accused murderer, who finds a homeless man that thinks that the defendant's lawyer is the actual murderer. That sounds absurd." Elliot lay back down and slid back into a sleeping position.

"Well, I don't care what you think. I'm going to the police."

"This is insane, Ruth. I won't argue with you. We'll speak tomorrow morning." Elliot turned on his stomach, hoping the pill's lingering effect would put him back to sleep. His wife was losing her senses from the stress.

Ruth did not sleep that night. She sat on the sofa drinking coffee, mentally rehearsing what she would say to the police in the morning. She thought about calling Mr. Barrett, but decided she would talk to the police first. She was furious. Elliot should at least consider what she was saying, not simply reject everything. She decided to speak to Detective Sills. He seemed to be a person who would take her seriously.

At six o'clock she got dressed and wrote a note to Elliot to tell him not to wait for her return. She would meet him later in the day at the courthouse. She took a taxi to the police station and demanded to see Detective Sills. The officer said he was still at home, and he would call to inform him of her urgent visit. She sat on a wooden bench and nervously awaited his arrival. She continued planning what to say, how to be effective, so she could convince Detective Sills to reopen the investigation. She wondered if she should have first gone by SoHo, so she could ask Stevie to come with her and support her story.

Detective Sills rushed out of his house learning of Ruth wanting to see him. He thought she was at the station to confess. He hoped the confession might be the turning point for successful closure of the case. *George was very effective and had probably made Ruth worried. A scorned wife is a great source of information*, he thought. As he entered the police station he saw Ruth standing in the hallway, anxiously awaiting his arrival.

"Good morning. Please come into my office."

"Good morning, detective. I'm sorry you had to wake up so early, but this is truly urgent."

"Oh, I'm an early riser, I don't require that much sleep. Would you like some coffee? I sure need some," he said, pouring coffee from the brewer.

"No. I'm anxious to talk to you."

"Are there some facts you want to share with me?" he said in a fatherly tone. "Some things you'll feel better confessing?"

"Confession? I came to tell you that Elliot did not do …"

"You woke me up that early to tell me that?" the detective said, completely disappointed.

Ruth gathered her thoughts and told him what she had discovered. He listened, but didn't seem at all excited.

"There are two possibilities," Sills said when she finished her story. "Either you are completely out of your mind with the stress of your situation, or this is a fantastic story that I cannot do anything about."

"What do you mean there's nothing you can do? You can re-open the investigation, you can speak to Stevie."

"Mrs. Barrett, please," Sills said in a somewhat condescending tone. "Come on. A homeless man tells you something that makes you believe that your husband's lawyer is really the killer? Please, doesn't it sound a little odd even to you?"

"Stevie is not the usual homeless person…" she said, resenting the detective's patronizing expression. "It does sound odd. Actually it sounds really crazy, but it's the truth. You have the wrong man. Ted fits the police profile. My husband does not."

"Someone with no credibility seeing a parked car is not a good reason for me to reopen a case that to my mind is already closed. If you don't like your husband's attorney, fire him. Don't involve me in a defamation suit."

"My husband is innocent of any wrongdoing and being wrongfully accused and you're worried about a lawsuit?"

"I'm worried about solving crimes. You must understand where I'm coming from. It's not so simple. You have nothing that justifies reopening this case."

"What if I give you more proof? What if I brought this witness in? Would that satisfy you? Would that make you reopen the investigation?"

"Yes, of course, of course." Sills said, thinking he would say anything to get this woman out of his office. He had seen some crazy wives with desperate ploys, but this one was completely out of her mind. *During the trial, she seemed intelligent. I would never have guessed she would turn completely nuts.*

Ruth was not defeated. She was onto something and nothing in the world would undermine her determination. She knew what she had to do. She took a taxi uptown and got out a few blocks from Ted's apartment. She entered a café with a view of Ted's building and ordered a cup of coffee. At 8:40 she saw him leave his building on his way to the courthouse. She walked across the street, asked the doorman to call Heather who invited her to come up.

"What's going on, Ruth? It's so early. Aren't you supposed to be in court?" Heather asked, half asleep and clearly surprised.

"I couldn't go today. I needed to talk to somebody," Ruth lied. "Elliot's family came to town and I needed… well I might need your help," she said quickly.

"There is coffee in the brewer, have a cup. Give me a few minutes to wash and get dressed," Heather said, disappearing into her bedroom.

I should have a better excuse, Ruth thought. *I must be very careful, I can't blow it.*

Ruth got up quietly and carefully, looked on the back of a few of the new paintings and at the base of some sculptures and found what she was looking for. Nirvana Gallery—Prince Street—SoHo, the address of Lindsey's gallery was stamped on the back. Her knees shook. She had enough evidence to tie Ted to the crime scene. She knew for certain that Ted had bought the paintings at Lindsey's gallery. He must have had an affair with her. She congratulated herself for remembering when Ted quickly changed the subject about the source of the paintings at the New Year's Eve party.

Now, Elliot is going to believe me and I have additional proof for Detective Sills. She tried to calm down, so Heather would not notice her agitation. After Heather finally finished dressing, Ruth stayed for ten minutes to support her excuse that she needed to talk, because she was stressed out about the court case. She pretended to listen to Heather's encouraging words, then left the apartment. On the street she thought of calling Elliot to tell him her findings, but then realized he was already in court.

In the courtroom that morning, Ted was surprised to see El-liot's parents and noted Ruth's absence. "Elliot, where's Ruth?" he asked.

"She'll probably be here this afternoon," Elliot shrugged his shoulders. Not really knowing what to make of Ruth's absence in light of what she'd told him the night before, he was worried about her.

During the day, Ted finished his rebuttal as the case moved toward closing arguments. Ted had already prepared his speech. He wanted to rehearse speaking it one more time, emphasizing the points he wished to impress upon the jury.

Elated, Ruth went back home, picked up her car and spent the rest of the morning searching for Stevie. He was not in the al-ley. She drove around SoHo and was relieved when she found him walking on the West Broadway and Houston. Stevie was surprised to see her and was glad to enter her car. Their encounter last night had aroused his curiosity. As they drove, Ruth explained what had happened to her husband and asked for his help.

Stevie thought it was one helluva story, but he didn't want to be involved. "I don't relate to the police or the judicial system. It has nothing to do with justice."

"I agree," Ruth said. "I almost lost my husband to the system, but there is another issue." She was searching for a way to help Ste-vie step away from his preconception. "This is an issue of truth. My husband doesn't deserve to be in jail while the guilty man is free. You're the only one that can help. Only you can shed light on this case. You need to talk to the detective. My words aren't enough."

Stevie was silent for a full minute. Then he looked at Ruth and grinned. "Well, when you put it that way…. Anyway, you've been very nice to me."

"What are you saying?" Ruth wanted to hear his confirmation.

"I owe you one. I'll help you, but don't be so sure the detective will believe me."

Ruth patted his knee in thanks. "Great. Now, I need you to do something else for me. I want to stop and buy you some new clothes."

Stevie was not willing. "I won't dress in a costume."

"Only blue jeans and a new shirt. You choose. How about it?" Ruth pleaded.

"OK. Blue jeans are cool. It's your money." They shopped at an Old Navy store. With his new clothes, Stevie looked more like a reliable witness. *Wish he would shave, but never mind now*, she thought.

They drove straight to Detective Sills' office without calling ahead. Sills was surprised to see Ruth return so soon.

Detective Sills listened to Stevie's account, and then questioned him about his background and about the details of what he had seen that night. *Definitely a street person, but he seemed credible*, Sills noted.

"Did you happen to see the Jaguar's license plate number?" he asked.

"As a matter of fact, yes. I did. The Jag had an unusual license plate that stuck in my mind. It was arrogant – Law-dash-Number-dash-One."

Ruth clapped her hands. "I can't believe it escaped my mind. I can't believe I didn't ask." Ruth remembered her disdain when last year, Ted drove to their home to show Elliot his new Jaguar and the new license plate.

Ruth then shared her discovery that Ted's new paintings and sculptures had come from Lindsey's gallery. She relayed Heather's story of how Ted had changed his behavior after Lindsey's murder and how he had long been a womanizer.

"Let me check out a few things and I will get back to you," Detective Sills said, a little taken back as he led them to the door. He immediately ordered a license plate check and a record check on Stevie. Then he called his team into his office.

Outside the police station Ruth hugged Stevie and thanked him for his help.

"What can I do for you in return?" Ruth asked.

"You don't owe me anything. I just said what I saw."

"Have you thought about the plan I proposed to you last night?"

"I'm considering it. Tell you what—I'll check out the art school to see if it's any good."

Ruth was curious about what was happening in the courtroom, but she was convinced it would all be irrelevant. She took Stevie to the art school on Eight Street in the Village. She followed him as he poked around and talked with some of the students as they left the building. The school offered workshops and classes to artists who were interested in discovering new modes of perception. He heard lot of talk about fostering an artist's personal growth. He seemed satisfied that the school's philosophy was not oppressive to individual creativity.

Afterwards, Ruth walked with Stevie for a few blocks to a four-story building her organization had rehabbed. The organization had acquired the building through an estate left without a family claim. She rummaged in her purse for the key to a small loft with a doorway to the building's roof. The loft was small but clean. Stevie seemed most interested in the natural light in the space. The roof area was large and had a great view of the Village. From there they could see other artists at work in the high-priced lofts that filled the neighborhood. *Would Stevie's pride keep him from living among them? Would he like sharing a building with the other recipients benefitting from the organization's grants?* He never spoke of accepting her offer, but she sensed Stevie was already beginning to feel at home there.

27

Everyone involved in a case eagerly awaits the day of closing statements. The witnesses have testified, the arguments have been made, the jury is tired, and it's time for the summation. Just as in the opening days of the trial, everyone tries to rise to the occasion. Ted bought a new suit, even more expensive than usual. George had a haircut, and as if trying harder, had carefully shaved. Elliot's tension was visible. He was glad the nightmare would be over, and blocked out all but optimistic thoughts about the outcome. Ruth had tried to get him to meet her mystery witness, but he was not interested. It was madness. He told Ruth that if she told any of her wild theories to his parents or mentioned them to Ted, it would mean the end of their marriage. He was surprised that she agreed with him.

Sitting next to Elliot's parents, Ruth seemed distant and detached from the drama, lost in her own thoughts. In fact, she was wondering what was happening with Detective Sills' investigation. *How much time would it take? When would he notify the judge?* Ruth wondered. Detective Sills had asked her and Stevie to keep things secret for the time being, so as not to create any interference with his new findings.

Judge Boyd seemed to join in the excitement and might even have shown a little smile for a short moment. The room was packed with anticipation.

George began with his closing statement. He had decided to risk a new approach. George spoke with frankness and conviction. "This is a serious matter that you, the jury, hold in your hands," he said, looking directly at each juror, "to finally deliberate and come up with a verdict in your journey for the truth." He tuned and pointed toward Elliot. "On the one hand, Elliot Barrett, a respected man, says he is innocent of the crime of murder. The defense would like you to believe that the state, the city, the police force, the district attorney and I are out to get Dr. Barrett; that we are here to disrupt his life and want to punish him for no apparent reason.

"Ladies and gentlemen, I can only speak for myself. I am not here to get anyone. I have no vendetta against Dr. Barrett; I am here to do my job. I can say with certainty that the police are not the enemy. I believe we did our job thoroughly. We brought many witnesses before you. We have gathered a preponderance of evidence for your consideration. We indisputably connected the defendant to the victim romantically. Sixty-five calls, does that strike you as reasonable to check to see if a mother took her medicine?" He paused, raising his eyebrows as if to dismiss such an absurd notion. He liked raising questions with self-evident answers that underscored his point. "We are not really talking here about the patient, Margaret Anderson, the bereaved mother. We are talking about her daughter, a beautiful woman, bright and full of vitality, a woman who was outgoing and could easily tempt any man under certain circumstances." He paused again for effect. "A woman we are certain was murdered by Dr. Elliot Barrett." He pointed at Elliot with a rebuking finger.

George went on to recount the evidence up to and during the night of the murder and the resulting investigation. "We have shown clearly and without dispute that Mr. Barrett's physical presence was all over the victim's apartment and that is indisputable." George knew that it was effective to keep repeating phrases that would stick in the mind of the jurors. "Of course, the defense will present all kinds of excuses as to why they were there. And I understand. That is the defense's job. I might even compliment the defense on doing a great job. But our task is not to judge flashy, skillful performances. Our task is to engage in an honest search for justice. I don't want you to convict an innocent man. Let me ask this question. Why didn't Elliot Barrett have the courage to stand before the jury and tell you his side of the story and then face cross examination?" George paused for dramatic effect, and then continued. "Ladies and gentlemen of the jury, the accused generally will not testify if he is hiding something. The law tells you that he need not testify. The defense would like you to believe it was a tactical decision and that there was no need for his testimony. I just don't buy that. An innocent person is eager to proclaim his innocence. Wouldn't you?"

George went on to discuss testimony of the expert psychologist. "You heard all of our esteemed experts. One said a man who has so much to lose might resort to a desperate act of violence." George recounted Elliot's qualifications and position. "The defendant comes from a respected, well-known family. He would not want to embarrass them. We all understand that. But what we cannot understand and cannot tolerate in a civilized society, is the taking of a human life to avoid embarrassment. We cannot tolerate acts of violence that end in death."

George referred to his opening statement, reminding the jury of his promise to deliver proof of Elliot's guilt. He knew he didn't have enough for murder in the first degree but believed Elliot would be convicted of second degree murder.

"We delivered everything we promised. Even the motive and the intent to murder. I do not have a question about that. Ladies and gentlemen, shortly you will begin your deliberations. Please do not compromise your vision. Take all the time you need. We are all eager to get back to our lives, but this may be the most important decision you will ever make. A man's life is in your hands. Justice for a woman whose life was cut tragically short is on your shoulders. If you find Mr. Barrett not guilty, then vote not guilty. I have no problem with that. But if you find him guilty, do not hesitate. Show him, and show society, hat we do not permit such actions. After all that you have seen in this courtroom there is only one verdict for this horrible crime. Guilty. Guilty without a doubt."

Reaction to the closing statement was divided. Some thought it was brilliant, original, effective and to-the-point. Others thought George missed the opportunity to jab at the defense. His intense but low-key approach might confuse the jury in believing he was not convinced of Elliot's guilt.

At first, Ted considered changing his closing statement to respond directly to George's style, but decided to stick to his original intention. He used a strong dramatic approach in attacking the police, the district attorney, and the authorities for a sloppy investigation and a weak prosecution. "The burden of proof offered by the prosecutor failed," he repeated many times. He said he had delivered on what he promised in his opening statement while the prosecution had not. He went through testimony after testimony, pointing failings of the prosecution's ability to make theory certain, to eliminate doubt. He pointed to all the mistakes the prosecution team made during the trial, trying to plant doubt in the minds of the jury. He took them through many plausible scenarios: the victim had been drunk, accidently killing herself. There was another assailant. He repeated testimony about Elliot's stellar record and career, and the statement "Dr. Elliot Barrett's life is all about life, not death." He pointed to Elliot's wife and parents and spoke of their place in society.

Ted glanced at Elliot at this point and was angry, but he hid his anger from the jury. He wanted the jury to view him with sympathy. Elliot sat motionless and tightlipped. Ted spoke affectionately of Ruth, a strong woman who believed her husband without doubt because she never had reason to doubt him. He was angry at her appearance. She seemed to be in a dream state, and he avoided any eye contact with her.

"Some of you may wonder why Dr. Barrett did not testify. The prosecutor would like you to believe it was a cowardly act. There is nothing farther from the truth. Dr. Barrett is a man of action and integrity, not of words. He is a doctor, not a speaker. On my advice he refrained from becoming a witness on the stand. In our system of justice, the burden of proof is on the prosecutor's side; the defense does not have to prove anything. The prosecution implied that my client has to prove he is not guilty. That is a deceptive statement like other deceptions you have heard from the other side. As a matter of fact, my client does not have to say anything, not even one word. It's the prosecution that must deliver on their promise to show proof beyond any doubt. They could not do so. They simply wanted my client on the stand to try to tarnish his reputation with wordplay and supposition, and I would not allow that to happen. My client's testimony was not necessary. Obviously he is not a murderer. The facts are clear. The police and the prosecution do not like to lose. No one likes to lose. They tried to convince you that it is somehow suspicious that we didn't do something we have no obligation to do." He again reminded the jury of Elliot's impeccable record as a doctor, a father, and a husband.

His final words were meant to leave a strong subliminal impression on their minds. "Ladies and gentlemen of the jury, I want you to remember as you deliberate that the life of an innocent man is in your hands. To this day, Ms. Margaret Anderson, Lindsey's mother, who inspired all of us by her strength, believes in Elliot's innocence. You heard her testimony in this courtroom. She heard the facts as presented by both sides, and was not confused. She, she still holds her strong conviction that Dr. Barret is innocent. As you deliberate, remember that just because the police want a conviction, just because society feels pressure to punish, we should not rush to judgment and put an innocent man in a place he does not belong."

The reaction of the media to Ted's final summation was not altogether favorable. Most of them thought Ted did not really respond to George's challenge. Instead he stuck to an old and ineffective strategy of attacking the police and the system. Ted's final statement was full of emotional drama but lacked originality, and it was too predictable. Most believed that Elliot should have appeared as a witness if he was innocent as he claimed, and allowed the jury to judge his performance.

Elliot's parents were not pleased with Ted's summation, believing he missed an opportunity to create a much stronger and effective impression in the minds of the jury. Elliot thought the speech was sufficient to win his acquittal. His faith in his friend remained strong. Ruth, who knew more than the others, thought Ted had played a game to manipulate the minds of the jury. His words had nothing to do with justice. She felt hatred toward Ted, whom she saw so clearly as a man able to lie without conscience. What kind of a person was he to stand in front of the world, lying through his teeth: putting his best friend in jail, in order to save his own skin? She wanted to stand up in front of everybody and expose him, but she did not want to tip her hand. She was planning to go to Detective Sills's office immediately after the jury began their deliberations to see when he would stop this fiasco.

The final statements ended early Wednesday afternoon. Judge Boyd was feeling frustrated as the gatekeeper, not the actual fact finder. At the end of each case, she was not allowed to state her opinion, only to instruct the jury before they began their deliberations. She explained the charges, and the details concerning the issue of the reasonable doubt and the difference between first-degree and second-degree murder. The jury was finally dismissed to start their deliberations.

"All rise," the court clerk announced. Judge Boyd loved the last announcements at the end of trials. She summarized the main portion of the arguments and ordered the jury to begin their work. The jury filed out and everyone began to await their verdict. No one knew how long the jury would deliberate. All hoped their side would win. If the prosecutor won, Sills would be praised and move closer to a promotion. If the defense lawyer won his reputation would grow, as would his financial reward. And, of course, there was the fate of the accused.

28

Twenty-eight days had passed since the beginning of the trial. Finally the jury could speak about the case among themselves. The pressure to keep their opinions bottled up and not to speak to anyone was demanding. Twelve jurors who sat through the whole trial listening to all the evidence now must render a verdict that would affect a man's fate forever.

The jury could be perceived as a metaphor of one mind with one body, deliberating about the many opposing forces and views in order to gain a clear consensus. It was not easy. They felt the load of responsibility weigh heavily on them. The case was not clear-cut. The defense and the prosecution had presented plausible scenarios. Opinions and theories were presented as fact, and facts were ridiculed as opinion and speculation. On the one hand the jurors did not want to convict an innocent man, but on the other hand they would not want to release someone with blood on his hands.

Right from the beginning Guyla Harrison, a high school teacher, exhibited leadership and was voted jury foreperson.

"I have a suggestion," she volunteered. "Before we waste our time deliberating let's take a preliminary vote, to see if we are already in agreement and save ourselves some time." The jury agreed and the vote was taken.

"Guilty or not guilty on the two counts?" she asked. Hands were raised; three for guilty, nine, not guilty. "O.K. We cannot agree completely. What about the first count of premeditative murder?" Nine jurors voted not guilty, three voted guilty.

"Second-degree?" Guyla announced. This time, ten jurors voted guilty, and two not guilty. "Okay then, let's begin deliberations on the first count," she said. They argued about the evidence. The main question was if the defendant had committed premeditated murder and went to Lindsey's apartment that night with the intention to kill her. After a few hours, the three minority jurors were convinced that there was sufficient doubt to assume that the murder was the result of the heat of the moment. The murderer has not brought a weapon with him. The evidence was circumstantial, at best.

On the second count, there were major disagreements. Two jurors felt Elliot was too respectable a man to be a murderer. They pointed to Mrs. Anderson as a reliable witness who surely had the strongest interest in the truth. One argued that Mrs. Anderson's testimony was charged with emotional prejudice that tainted her judgment. A woman juror said that Elliot's behavior in the courtroom showed his guilt. "An innocent man does not act so depressed and behave as if he was a rock. He should show some fighting instinct," she opined.

"He is a doctor who is not in his element," another juror replied.

"Well, if he had testified, we all could have a better way of knowing what happened," another said.

"He did not have the obligation to do so," said another.

The arguments went back and forth for hours, until Guyla said they should proceed witness by witness and stick to arguing the main points. "This is not a black or white case. Both sides argued well. We're the scale. We should weigh the two sides and see which side has the weight of truth. Then we can make an intelligent decision." The jury had a hard time choosing which arguments were the more convincing. Both sides had presented good arguments, and it was almost impossible to know with certainty who was telling the truth and who was only making a good argument.

Reasonable doubt was also a difficult concept to understand. Everything seemed negotiable and needed to be balanced—to be perceived not only logically but also emotionally.

Many questions were raised and the arguments grew fierce. "Was the body moved or not?" one juror asked. Although they were told by Judge Boyd not to consider that testimony, it still puzzled them. Did Detective Sills have total reliability, or was he coloring the facts? That topic raised another heated discussion. A few jurors argued that the police could never be trusted. They believed the police acted from pressure to solve crimes, especially murder cases, and could set up a defendant, or just look at facts in their investigation that favored their case. Others denied that this was happening in this particular investigation. They asked to see the transcript that dealt with this issue and went over it line by line.

Could they rely on the waitress to be an accurate judge of the degree of friendliness between the victim and the doctor? What if she saw their behavior through her own desirous eyes? Was Elliot really having an affair? They thought it was probable, based on the high number of telephone conversations presented in evidence.

A vigorous discussion arose over the testimony of the psychological witness. Was the testimony opinion or fact? "All those psycho experts say is a bunch of hogwash, presumed experts whose information comes from books," one older juror argued. "They come to the courtroom as if they know everything about humans. They don't know shit."

"If they're experts, how come they oppose each other's opinions? If a study is scientific then results are uniform," another juror said.

"They are learned men," the youngest juror said. "That's why they were called to testify."

"If they're so expert, how come they disagree?" The older man repeated, determined to have the last word on the subject.

"The interesting point about expert testimony is who brought a better expert and who was paid more for their testimony," another juror added.

"But Dr. Rosenthal did not get paid," another juror argued.

"Who knows what his motive was. Come on, don't tell me that

someone will spend so much time to come and testify just because of justice."

"We're here for justice. The money we're given is nothing."

"Yes, but that's different…"

"No it's not."

"Yes it is…"

"Come on guys. We're getting away from the main issue," Guyla interrupted. "Let's cut the personal attacks."

"Yes, someone could end up dead," the older man said, to a tension-revealing round of laughter. "I'm surely not going to volunteer to be a juror at that trial," someone continued—which made everyone laugh.

On Friday morning the jury showed signs of weariness. Guyla tried to resolve the differences, and on most points they came to some agreement. On the rest, they went back to the transcript to reread the arguments. "Let's try to reach an agreement today, so we can have the weekend free with this court case behind us," Guyla challenged. "We have come so far. There are only a few points left to consider and then we can come to unanimous agreement."

"We should not be put under pressure to finish before the weekend. A man's life is on the line and we have a heavy responsibility to come up with a just verdict," the youngest juror insisted. She had doubts that Elliot was involved in the murder.

"Fine, let's stay another six months…"

"Guys, guys. Don't start with that kind of sarcastic remark. It won't get us anywhere," Guyla cautioned.

While the jury was deliberating, Detective Sills continued his investigation.

He spent the day checking the gallery's telephone records, a detail that had completely escaped his mind. He found that Ted had placed more calls to Lindsey than Elliot had. Motor vehicle records confirmed that Ted's red Jaguar had the vanity license plate Stevie had described. A detailed search located a Thai restaurant near the gallery that had three take-out orders recorded that night paid for with Ted's credit- card signature.

The detective painfully admitted that his focus on Elliot at the beginning of the investigation had prevented him from looking into other possibilities. He even wondered if someone in the past had also suffered from his rush to judgment. He excused his behavior because of the strange coincidence that both men know the same woman so well— maybe both having affairs with her.

Was I too eager to find a victim and get my superior off my back for a quick result? The thought plagued him all day. He dreaded the moment when he would have to go to his superior to explain that he might have made a major mistake. Sills tried to construct theories that would allow him to dismiss the new evidence. He considered himself a moral man. In his many years as an officer of the law, he had developed a strong sense of duty, wanting to bring the right person to justice. A few times in the past, he had crossed the line when dealing with hard criminals, when he knew for certain that his suspect was guilty.

Ruth had called many times and showed up at his office unannounced, wanting to know where things stood. She begged him to hurry and reach a conclusion. She offered her help with anything he needed, but he told her she had done more than enough. She told him she was in agony, keeping this all of this important information to herself. He admired this unrelenting woman whose love for her husband had driven her to an instinctive series of actions that may have led her to find the real killer. He explained to her he was waiting for the forensic reports to make his findings conclusive.

The report came back positive; Ted's hair was found among the physical evidence collected by the technicians at Lindsey's apartment. Now with the physical evidence tying Ted to the crime scene, Sills had the confidence needed to go to his superior to explain the bizarre twist of events.

At his office, Ted waited anxiously for the call from the court clerk to announce the jury's verdict. The longer they deliberated, the higher chance they would convict Elliot. Ted felt he had done a good job, but he had not struck a decisive blow to undermine the opposition. Waiting for the final decision was nerve-wracking. He pushed all thought of Elliot's innocence out of his mind and worried about the verdict.

He sensed something was wrong with Ruth and Elliot. Theirs was not the overly-stressed situation he had witnessed in other clients. Ruth had bombarded him with questions, but, for the last few days, she had stopped communicating with him. He didn't know what to make of Ruth's sudden visit to his home. Heather insisted Ruth just needed to talk. Nothing unusual had happened, just women talking, and she had stayed no more than ten minutes. His lawyer's instinct mad him suspicious. However, his mind was too full of worries to focus on any detail—even one that could be his undoing.

29

Ruth's patience with Detective Sills had reached its limit. She was afraid the jury would end its deliberations before he finished his investigation. She threatened to go to his superior. He told her there were only a few small matters to clear up and to wait for his call. Within the hour she called again. "I have a feeling the jury is going to come out with a verdict before the weekend" Ruth said nervously.

"I sympathize with your anxiety. I have almost everything added up. I promise to call you by noon."

Elliot returned from the clinic that day after only two hours of work. He said he couldn't work well under all the stress and pressure. Ruth invited Elliot's parents for lunch. They sat in the dining room discussing the case and its probable outcome when the telephone rang. Everyone jumped. "It's the jury, they're finished," Elliot's mother shouted her guess nervously.

Ruth dashed to the phone, turning her back to her family. "Hello. This is Detective Sills. I promised I would call you as soon as possible. I am going right now to relay my finding about Ted to my superior. Your suspicions may prove to be absolutely right."

"Who is it?" Elliot asked anxiously.

Ruth's heart was pounding. She pointed her finger at Elliot, signaling for him to wait a minute. "You don't know how happy you've made me. Thank you," she said as she placed the phone back on its cradle. The excitement was apparent in her glowing face.

"Yes!" she shouted.

They all jumped to their feet. "What in the hell is going on?" Mr. Barrett asked.

Ruth recounted the whole story. She started with her meeting with Stevie and her failed attempt to talk to Elliot. They bombarded her with questions, wanting to make sure it was not just a suspicion.

"Why did you keep it a secret from us?" Mr. Barrett asked, still reeling from what he just heard.

"I tried to tell Elliot… Detective Sills asked me not to tell anyone. He thought…"

"Even from us?" Mrs. Barrett asked, incredulously.

"This is unbelievable." Mr. Barrett was still bewildered. "I need to call my lawyer right away to see what to do now." Mr. Barrett took the phone out of his pocket and dialed his attorney's number. He was frustrated when he could not speak to Mr. Bernstein and left an urgent message with his secretary.

Elliot was stunned and still seemed doubtful. "This is impossible, this is impossible," he repeated.

"Never mind impossible. It's the truth. I've just spoken to the detective," Ruth said, agitated.

The telephone rang again and Ruth ran to pick it up. Ted was calling.

"Ruth, the jury has just finished deliberations. Judge Boyd is ordering everyone back to the courthouse."

Ruth hung up the phone wordlessly. What did this mean? What were they to do? When she told Elliot and his parents about the call, they were also confused.

"Where in heaven's name is my lawyer?" Mr. Barrett said. "The case is over. We do not need to go to the courthouse. All they need to do is arrest that bastard!"

Elliot was silent. Ruth called Detective Sills and told him about the call from Ted. The detective told her they should proceed to the courthouse. He was still trying to obtain a warrant for Ted's arrest.

In the car ride to the courthouse, the Barretts talked almost non-stop. "That son of a bitch," Mr. Barrett shouted. "I never liked that son of a bitch. Ruth, you never liked him either, did you?"

"I never liked him," Ruth agreed.

Elliot had withdrawn into himself and did not share the excitement. His parents assumed he was in shock, or feeling horribly betrayed by his best friend.

What an odd reaction from Elliot, after hearing such happy news for the second time, Ruth thought.

"Elliot," Mrs. Barrett said, "I thought you would be so happy."

Elliot looked at her feeling dazed. "Leave me alone, Mother. Ted is my best friend. I don't believe this."

"At least be happy that you are out of trouble," Mrs. Barrett said.

Ruth was angry. "You want more proof, Elliot? Detective Sills has evidence that Ted was involved in the killing. What else do you need to know?"

"They also had evidence on me," Elliot said, as he turned away to stare out the window. When they arrived at the courthouse, they found it difficult to climb the stairs because of the crush of reporters and television crews blocked their way and shouted questions. They did not respond and slowly forced their way up to the courtroom.

Elliot sat down next to Ted, as the Barretts and Ruth searched frantically for Detective Sills. Ted tried to make eye contact with Elliot, but his eyes looked downward as he took his seat. "Hey Elliot, don't be such a pessimist," he said, which got no response from Elliot. The clerk called for everyone in the court to rise and Judge Boyd entered from her chamber as the jury began filing in from a separated door. After Judge Boyd asked the required questions the foreman rose to announce the verdict: guilty of murder in the second degree.

Time seemed frozen when, with a loud burst through the double doors, Detective Sills arrived, followed by two uniformed officers. They headed straight to the judge's bench. To everyone's surprise he announced, "I am here to proclaim the need to interrupt these proceedings immediately."

Judge Boyd looked furious at his interruption. "Detective Sills, approach the bench at once." She then instructed the astonished jury to leave the room.

The courtroom was hushed. All eyes were on the detective and the judge. Her face revealed nothing, all her attention on the documents produced by Detective Sills. After a few minutes, during which she studied the documents closely, she leaned back, folded her arms and announced, "Proceed."

To the profound astonishment of almost everyone in the courtroom, the detective and the officers moved to the defense table and began to read Ted his rights. They were arresting him on suspicion of murder.

"I call for a recess," Ted said loudly, and somewhat irrationally. His mind was racing. He had feared this moment, but he had never imagined it at such an inopportune time. Earlier in the day, when he learned that the jury had completed their deliberations, he felt a sense of relief the trial was ending.

Judge Boyd banged her gavel and said, loudly and pointedly, "The court declares a recess until Monday morning. Please instruct the jury of the new charges," she said to the court clerk.

Everyone watched with bewilderment as Benjamin Sills handcuffed Ted. Mr. and Mrs. Barrett screamed at Ted, blaming him for all their anguish. After the judge left the bench no one in the courtroom tried to restore order. Elliot sat down and seemed frozen. He stared straight ahead as if struck by lightning. Ted managed to keep his composure. He tried to explain that the charge against him was mistake, as the police led him away.

The courtroom reporters used their phones, briefing their news desks on the astonishing developments. The prosecution team watched the drama unfold, as shocked as everyone else. They were hoping for a guilty announcement from the jury. George was furious that he was not informed of the new development beforehand. His anger turned into self-examination of his role. He had worked hard to convince the jury that Elliot was the killer. *How could it be that Elliot is innocent? All the evidence clearly pointed toward him. The physical evidence, the car, the eye-witnesses, the experts. I was almost an instrument for convicting an innocent man.* Now his legal victory seemed hollow. *It seemed that this had all been a game of who was a better lawyer. How could this crazy arrest be valid?* George started to doubt the whole judicial system. *Had an innocent man been convicted? Who would believe that Ted had murdered Lindsey? What if Sills has made a terrible mistake? Sills would not take such a chance. This is all too crazy.*

George ducked out the door and rushed to his office trying to unravel the bizarre twist of events.

30

During the drive to the police station Ted tried to determine his next move. *Should I call a lawyer at this point? No, I'm going to insist there is no need at all.* He was not going to make it easy for the police. By denying involvement with the murder. *What does Benjamin Sills have on me—what Ruth uncovered by snooping around? Was it my paintings? I should have hidden them right after the New Year party. Does Heather have anything to do with it? No, that's not possible.*

Ted felt the tight grip of the handcuffs as he followed Sills into the police station. The news of his arrest had spread quickly and he felt humiliated as everyone stopped what they were doing to look at him as he passed by. Ted was escorted through the regular round of being fingerprinted and photographed, then the officer led him to a holding cell. For the first time he experienced the degradation so many of his clients had experienced. *It was Elliot who had to endure that kind of humiliation. I will never be able to look Elliot in the eyes again.*

A few minutes later, an officer led Ted into an interrogation room. Detective Sills had not wasted any time. He wanted to take advantage of Ted's shock, hoping to benefit from his weakness. Ted had been in the interrogation room many times, but always as an attorney. This time he was the one under arrest.

"Do you want to have a lawyer present?" Detective Sills asked, knowing he must play this one strictly by the book.

Ted kept his cool. "There is no need for a lawyer."

"Do you have a statement you wish to make at this point?"

"What in hell am I doing here?"

"Do you have any feelings about what you did to your lover?

What you did to your best friend?" Sills tried the guilt angle, knowing it worked sometimes.

Ted was defiant. "You are making a big mistake, detective. You will have to pay for it dearly."

"I accept my responsibility. Why don't you accept yours?" Sills jabbed back, realizing that he'd let Ted agitate him. The first unwritten rule in an investigation was always to be in control of a situation, never led by emotion. He realized he was angry at himself for jumping too quickly to conclusions regarding Elliott's guilt.

"I have nothing to say to you."

"As you wish."

Sills stared at Ted and shrugged off a small flicker of doubt. This time he had the right man. With a soft voice he changed his tactic from a logical and sensible approach into an emotion-based statement. Sills knew that the normal desire of people was to avoid pain and gain pleasure. "Ted, I know you are a smart person. I feel for you. I know it's humiliating to be arrested. I do not draw any pleasure from this and I apologize for your inconvenience. I have spent the last few days finding facts that connect you to the crime scene. After you answer a few questions for me, I will not object to a bail request. But this charge against you can't be wished away."

"I did not do anything wrong. You know that. You made the same mistake with me as you made with Elliot. Or maybe his father wrote you a big check? I'll be damned if I'll answer your questions."

"Regretfully, you are making the wrong choice," Sills said, and called a guard to take the suspect back to his cell.

Ted knew he needed legal counsel, but he was arrogant enough to want to map out a strategy before he summoned an attorney. He would keep his silence and play a waiting game. But first he needed to know what Detective Sills had on him.

Later that night, a guard led Ted back to the interrogation room. *They are not going to intimidate me*, Ted thought. *I know all their tricks. It's not going to work with me.* He sat down, well aware that Sills was watching him through the one-way mirror. Like a poker player he showed no emotion, no clue to his turmoil and guilt.

Sills knew Ted would be a hard nut to crack. This was a man who knew the law inside and out, a man who had hidden his own guilt, willing to send his best friend to prison. Sills planned to use the advanced technique he first learned in the army where he had served as a military interrogator. He did use this technique only on rare occasions using suggestions—embedded commands—that spoke to the subconscious.

Sills walked into the interrogation room and asked Ted in a soft voice. "If you want to tell the truth or not tell the truth that is entirely up to you." The command to tell the truth was spoken at a slightly higher pitch in order to force its effectiveness into Ted's subconscious. Sills exhaled his cigarette smoke at the same time to distract Ted's conscious mind.

"I know my rights," Ted said.

"You can tell me, thereby by freeing yourself from the heavy burden you are carrying. If you feel it would be for your benefit and you think I want to help you, then just say it. You will realize it's the right decision to unload your guilt and tell me the truth."

Sills didn't realize that Ted was studying him. He understood Sills intentions all along. As in a poker game, when there is what is called a 'tell' – Sills had revealed his unconscious purpose.

"I didn't do anything wrong, and I don't have a statement for you," Ted repeated.

The interrogation continued, with Sills using every trick he had learned from his long career. He knew it would be hard for Ted to change his mind because he would consider it failure and weakness. Sills tried to invoke strong emotions in Ted, hoping his perception of reality would become clouded. He hoped he would slip up and make a mistake that would condemn him. They were conducting a mind game in which Ted had nothing to lose and consequently, he was not vulnerable to Sills' efforts to penetrate his defense. Ted rejected any attempt to tie him to the crime by refusing to answer any questions regarding his involvement with Lindsey. He knew that the information Sills possessed would not necessarily be accepted as proof in a court of law.

After a guard led Ted back to his cell, he lay down and fell into a deep sleep. He had been exhausted playing the game. A uniformed officer awakened Ted and told him that someone had made put up bail for him. After collecting his belongings he was led into a waiting area where he saw Heather pacing slowly. She had come to take him home. As Heather drove uptown, the early Saturday morning streets were empty of traffic. Ted appreciated her almost complete silence. At the apartment, she made coffee and sat across from him. She finally broke the silence. "What is going on, Ted? I am utterly confused."

Despite all the help she had provided, Ted was not ready to face Heather. "I need a little time for myself right now. I need to clear my mind."

Heather drew her lips into a tight line. Wordlessly, she placed her cup and saucer in the sink. "From now on, it's going to different around here. I need to know what is going on."

"I promise I will get back to you, and tell you all the truth."

Heather stomped out of the room. *I'll not wait too long*, she thought.

Ted sat at his desk, opened the Post and read the new facts and rumors about his arrest. *I should look into hiring a good lawyer. Can't afford to waste any time.*

He spread Elliot's file over his desk and tried to focus his thoughts. *First the alibi. I was home at 9:30. The medical examiner made a mistake estimating the time of death between 9:30 and 10:45 P.M. Heather could testify that I was home at 9:30.* He tried to think who else saw him that night and remembered the doorman on duty in his building.

He wrote a note to investigate that point.

As Ted studied the file, something emerged from one of the pages that left him with an uncanny sensation. It was the gruesome photograph of Lindsey's body. Ted picked it up and had the courage to examine it for the first time. He saw something now that had escaped his attention when he had previously glanced at the pho-tograph. There was makeup on her face. To make sure, he took a magnifying glass to examine the photograph more closely. He was astonished by what he saw.

He sat for a long time, wondering how this evidence fit with the fact that her position on the couch had also altered. *All along, I thought it was lousy work during the first night of investigating the crime scene. Her mother could have moved her face, but she definitely didn't put makeup on her face. Could it be that Lindsey was not dead when I left her that night? Having regained consciousness could she have put on makeup? Could I have been in such a panic that I didn't notice that she was still alive?* Ted held his head in his hands, feeling pressure and confusion, still not knowing what to make of the new discovery. *I had left in a hurry. Didn't make sure of anything, except to remove all signs of my presence. Perhaps the medical examiner was right when he claimed the time of death was at least half an hour after I left the apartment. Did Lindsey get up, become dizzy and fall down again? Was she that drunk? No... that was impossible. Sills and the medical examiner testified that she was suffocated with a pillow. How to explain the makeup? How and why did she put on makeup after I left?*

Ted's eyes were darting behind closed lids. Too many thoughts were rushing through his mind. *If the medical examiner were right...* he forced himself to think clearly.

What if Lindsey had been suffocated, and had not died by hitting her head as I had thought? Lindsey was suffocated...Suffocated! Ted burst out, shouting, "Then I am innocent!"

Heather rushed to Ted's desk and found him bewildered and ecstatic. "What is going on, Ted? You look like you just saw a ghost."

"I did, I see a ghost... No. Actually, I smell a rat."

"A rat. How disgusting. What in the hell are you talking about?"

"Someone must have been in the apartment after I left ..." Ted mumbled.

"What are you saying? I don't understand you."

"Heather, please. Not now. I am in the middle of making an unbelievable discovery."

Heather left the room hurt and angry.

Ted was developing a theory to fit these new discoveries. He was trying hard to regain his concentration. *Maybe one of Lindsey's many lovers came over and killed her for who knows what reason. How could he know with certainty how many lovers she had? Maybe someone bought drugs from someone.* He discounted that theory. *Lindsey was too sharp to have a drug habit. And jealousy aside, she said the only other man she had been seeing was Elliot.*

Ted started pacing the room. He tried to quiet his mind so he could think straight. A nagging need to go to the bathroom demanded immediate attention. He rushed to the bathroom and sat on the commode. Trying to relax, he flushed the toilet and with the sound of the rushing water, his body awareness returned, and he felt the pleasure of finally being relieved.

The confined room seemed to force his mind to focus, and an exclamation came to him in a flash of clarity. *George's theory, his witness testimonies and his arguments were right, after all.* It took a minute for the full weight of these insights to penetrate Ted's mind. "It was Elliot!" Ted shouted. "Son of a bitch, it was Elliot. The last person on earth I would have suspected. I knew all along he had an affair with Lindsey. She must have called him after I left her apartment, when she regained consciousness. Lindsey put on makeup before Elliot arrived at her apartment that night. It was Elliot after all. That son of a bitch," he yelled, banging his body against the wall.

"Are you all right?" Heather knocked on the door, worried about Ted. "What did Elliot... you must tell me right now." Ted opened the door and pulled Heather onto the couch. "Heather, you won't believe what I just figured out. Elliot murdered Lindsey."

"What? But the television..."

"I know. I know," Ted said impatiently. "I was almost fooled myself because..."

"Don't keep me in the dark any longer," she protested. "I must know what you're thinking."

"Please, Heather. Give me an hour. I promise to give you my

complete attention in one hour."

"One hour. Not more," she warned.

Ted returned to his desk and examined all the evidence again. This time he put everything in chronological order. He typed frantically on his laptop, organizing the events as he now understood them. When he finished, he printed the outline and read it over carefully. He had left Lindsey's apartment at 9:05 P.M. That was when Stevie saw him. Lindsey must have been murdered between 9:30 to 10:45; that time period was established correctly by the medical examiner. She had regained consciousness soon after he left, and probably she had called Elliot shortly thereafter. She had applied her makeup while waiting for Elliot's arrival. It took Elliot approximately thirty minutes to arrive. That time line confirmed Mr. Blumenthal's testimony. He said he saw Elliot's Mercedes at around 10:00.

The theory Sills and George had constructed was actually very accurate. The only missing link was why Lindsey and Elliot had fought each other. Did she tell him about Ted, the way she had told Ted about Elliot? Did Elliot try to end the affair and then flew into a rage when Lindsey threatened to tell Ruth? Would Lindsey threaten to do something like that? *I know how that son of a bitch guards his family's reputation,* Ted thought, and his old anger surfacing again. *Now I understand why he was so depressed during the trial. I thought he felt bad because he was lying to his fucking wife. I never could stand her ass.* Ted's anger grew. He was tempted to call Elliot and Ruth and dump all his discoveries on them, but he knew he had to be clever and not do anything based on his emotional state.

He thought of calling Sills to report what he had just discovered, but that would mean admitting his own affair and admitting that he had allowed another man to be tried for a murder Ted believed for months that he had committed.

31

Heather stood looking over Ted's shoulder for a few moments before he noticed her. He jumped up instinctively, surprised. "How long have you been standing there?"

"Just for a few minutes. You were deep in thought; I was waiting for you to notice me. An hour has passed. I'm ready now to hear your side of the story."

Ted also was ready to speak. "Heather, sit down. Everything that happened on the   night of Lindsey's murder is clear to me now. I want to be completely honest with you. I want to tell you everything, without hiding a thing. I'll face the consequences. Before the trial, our relationship was not going well." Ted took a deep breath before he continued. "It's true what the reporters have being saying about my affair with Lindsey."

Heather's face grew pale. She knew that Ted had cheated, but with Lindsey, the murdered woman?

"Did you kill Lindsey?" she asked in a whisper.

"No, no, I didn't."

"How can I trust you, Ted? You haven't been truthful with me in the past," she shouted angrily.

"You must believe me. I'm telling you the truth." Ted explained the events of the night Lindsey was murdered, and what had taken place up until his arrest.

Heather was struck silent by the revelations of deceit and betrayal from both Ted and Elliot. "That's why you have been nice to me recently," she said sarcastically. "You only think of yourself. We were going to get a divorce, but then you discovered I was a good alibi. And what kind of a friend are you to Elliot? My god, this is unbelievable."

"Please Heather, sit down."

"I'm leaving this crazy house," she screamed. She felt a burning pain in her stomach. What Ted had told her was too much to bear.

Ted followed her to the bedroom, watching her pack her suitcase. "I didn't kill Lindsey. Heather, don't leave me now. I need you more now than I have ever needed anybody in my entire life."

"It's too late for that," she said, not looking at him.

"We've had a great relationship the past few months, haven't we?" Ted asked persuasively.

"It was all a lie," she said. "You are not capable of a relationship. I don't think our relationship can ever be restored." She kept throwing clothes into the suitcase without really paying attention to what she was packing. She was surprised that she was not crying. She felt a sudden surge of strength. She was doing what she decided to do, without the need for approval from anyone.

"Where will you go? Why not stay in the other room while you rest and think it over?"

"I'm no longer your concern. I'll stay at my parents' house for a short time until I decide what I want to do next."

"I understand. I deserve everything coming to me. Just know that when this mess is over, I'll do anything I can to get us back together."

To Heather, his words sounded empty. She carried her suitcase to the elevator, refusing Ted's help. She asked the doorman to summon a taxi to take her to the airport. She did not respond to Ted's goodbye or his pleas for her to call him and let him know she had arrived safely.

Ted spent the rest of the evening sitting in his chair, paralyzed, without the will to get up to turn on a light in the darkened apartment. He felt the utter despair and loneliness of being abandoned. Could it be that he really did love his wife? Was he just being emotional?

I must decide my next course of action. I cannot afford the leisure of not taking action to prove my innocence. He still was unable to move from his chair. Then, something else hit him hard. *I cannot speak about the case or my new revelations. There is the issue of lawyer-client privilege. I cannot tell Sills what I know because of the lawyer-client secrecy.* Ted couldn't remember a similar case that he could consult to clarify this issue.

He fought feelings of hopelessness and desperation, knowing he had to do something to save himself. The only course of action that emerged was to talk to Judge Boyd; after all, she was the judge in Elliott's case. *Old cranky granny could cook me for dinner.* He picked up the phone and called the judge at home before he could talk himself out of it.

Judge Boyd was enjoying the beginning of a quiet Saturday evening. Her two grandchildren had just left after spending a fun-filled afternoon in Central Park where she had taken them and her dog, Brandy. She enjoyed watching the children skating in the park while Brandy ran along the edge of the ice rink. She was remembering the chaotic events that took place in the courtroom on Friday when the phone rang.

"Hello, is this Judge Boyd's residence?" She was surprised to hear Ted's hesitant voice on the line.

"Yes, this is Meredith Boyd."

"This is Ted Lapoltsky... I was wondering if it would be possible to visit you tonight."

"Tonight? Can't you wait until Monday?"

"Please...it is a very urgent matter."

Judge Boyd heard the urgency in Ted's voice, but she was worried about inviting a murder suspect to her home. Curiosity got the best of her, and she invited Ted to come to her apartment at 8:30. She wasn't likely to become a victim of a crime of passion.

This is the most bizarre situation I've ever witnessed in my courtroom, she thought. *Lapoltsky was pompous to the extreme, but a murderer?* Judge Boyd drifted back into her reverie. At times, she felt the urge to retire and devote more time to her family and other interests she had neglected. *I love the mental task in the court which I have viewed as a pleasurable challenge, but there are also boring days when court procedures seem to go on forever.* She always felt she could render better verdicts than any jury, but in this case, she was completely wrong. She believed Elliot was guilty, and the new turn of events challenged her confidence. This case was truly exceptional.

Ted arrived on time. Judge Boyd, wearing a cardigan sweater hanging loosely over her jeans, welcomed him in. Brandy stayed beside her and greeted Ted with friendly barks. Judge Boyd led Ted into her living room.

"I'm going to make some tea. Would you like some, or would you prefer coffee?"

"Tea is fine, thanks," Ted was surprised by Boyd's appearance. She was relaxed and pleasant. At home, the design of her ultra-modern rooms and her much softer demeanor was unanticipated. He hadn't expected that the contrast between courtroom and home would be so dramatic. Her dog was friendly. He put a paw on Ted's knee, asking to be petted. "You surely don't have any worries," Ted said as he patted his rump.

Judge Boyd came back from the kitchen and laid a wooden tray on the table. "You can add your own sugar," she said. "So what kind of mess did you get yourself involved in? And why are you here?"

"I desperately need to speak to someone. I thought you would be able to help me." He told her all he had discovered—his relationship with Lindsey, the events of her last night, his mistake in thinking he was responsible for Lindsey's death. He spoke about Elliot being his nemesis, of their past friendship and of the depths of his envy. He couldn't believe she would listen to his story for so long and with such interest, but once he began he couldn't stop. He told Judge Boyd that he did attempt to provide Elliot with a good defense. She lowered her eyes as if this part of his confession was just too implausible.

"I have been completely honest with you, Judge Boyd, so you

can believe the unbelievable. One, I found out that I was not responsible for Lindsey's death. Two, I am certain Elliot is the murderer."

Judge Boyd was fascinated by the complexities Ted had revealed. She listened intently to what Ted had said. She knew it took great courage for Ted to speak so frankly. "You have a real problem on your hands," she said. "There is the issue of attorney-client privilege. You'll be searching for precedents on that one for days. You do have the fundamental right to defend yourself but…."

"I don't know what to do. I thought you might be able to shed some light."

"There are many issues, Ted. You agreed to defend someone in a case in which you personally were involved. You know better than that. No one is going to rush to believe you now. Your ethics have been shattered in several ways."

"Yes, I know. I have no excuse for my actions except stupidity. I panicked and every action after that reflected the original actions."

"And selfishness, Ted. That has played a big role in this. Now let's concentrate on the present. Come clean. Go to the police and tell them everything you know. They won't believe a word at first, but they will investigate. They have to."

"Isn't it ironic that throughout my career as a lawyer I always advised clients against talking to the police?"

"As a whole, the judicial system works well. Occasionally, maybe a few criminals go free but most of the time justice is served. You still have an advantage—you know the law. When you come clean to everyone, your conscience will be clear and you can better handle whatever consequences you'll have to endure."

Ted let her words sink in. He patted the dog lying at his feet. "You really make me think, Judge Boyd."

"No soft soap, Lapoltsky." She smiled and picked up the tea tray.

"Can I ask you one more question?"

"Ask away, but then we must call it a night. Cranky grannies need their rest."

"You know what we…?"

"Yes, I know what you call me. Never forget, in the courtroom all judges wear masks to give order and respectability to the institution of justice. But we all… most of us… have our human sides. What's your question, counselor?"

Ted smiled. He was touched by her sincere words. "I withdraw the question, Judge. I'll just thank you and say goodnight."

32

Driving home from Judge Boyd's house turned out to be hazardous. Icy sleet made the roads slippery. Ted had to drive slowly, cautiously. Five blocks from his apartment, the driver of a car in front of him applied the brakes unexpectedly and started to skid, swirling from side to side. Ted pumped his own brakes while turning the wheel in the opposite direction in an attempt to avoid collision. These tactics failed and he heard a hollow sound and as he smashed into the car in front of him, crumbling the Jaguar's front fender. His heart skipped a beat as the car's airbag inflated, throwing his head back forcefully. He felt some nausea from the smell of the preservative powder escaping from the airbag.

Two men emerged from the car he had hit and helped him leave his car. They asked if he was injured. Trying to balance himself on the icy road, he told them he felt a dull pain in his ribs. Otherwise, he was fine. He inspected the Jag and realized it was so damaged he would not be able to drive home.

The long wait for the tow company to arrive was agony. He held his cell phone, thinking he'd call someone to pass the time, but realized he had no one to call.

Lindsey was dead. Heather had left. His relationship with Elliot was over forever.

Sitting in his car chilled, his entire life passed through his mind. He had relentlessly pursued power, money and women. Perhaps it was time to rethink his goals.

Finally, the truck arrived and towed away his car. He wished he had asked for a ride to his apartment. There were no cabs to be found. Walking on the icy road was difficult. He was not dressed properly, and he felt the chilling cold penetrate his bones.

The freezing sleet and cold wind burned his eyes and his tears blurred the dark road.

Past midnight, Ted arrived home, exhausted. He crashed into bed, hoping to fall asleep. He tossed and turned for a few hours, still feeling the cold. The conversation with Judge Boyd continued to play in his mind. He knew the consequences of his actions would cost him dearly. If he came clean, he'd probably be disbarred. At the least, he would face more humiliation by confessing to Detective Sills and having to face his family, his colleagues and his acquaintances. *What have I done to myself?* He recalled the regrettable moment when he ran, in panic, from Lindsey's apartment. *What kind of animal are you?* Ruth's yelling in the courtroom echoed in his mind. The pain of Heather leaving him alone without bothering to look at him or respond to his plea to stay hit him like a rock. Ted's world felt empty and dark.

At six o'clock Sunday morning, he got out of bed, accepting the idea that the only way out of his misery was to confess to Sills. With a heavy heart, he called the police station and arranged a meeting for eight o'clock.

Ted found Sills waiting in his office. His heart was pounding fast, as he said to Sills, "I'm here to tell you the whole truth."

That will be the day, Sills thought. *What tactic does he have up his sleeve this time?* He observed Ted closely, trying to determine his intent. Ted had proved to be a good actor. This time, his unshaven face looked weary. "Do you want to have a lawyer present?" Sills asked. He had interrogated a few criminals who knew they had the right to be silent, yet they felt compelled to confess. Later in court, their lawyers attempted to dispute their confession, saying it was taken under duress.

"There's no need for that."

"Is it all right if I use a tape recorder?" Sills knew he must cover his bases.

"I have no problem with that," Ted said, knowing full well that any decent lawyer would advise the contrary, because in the courtroom it was very hard to dispute recorded statements in the courtroom.

In his long career, Sills had watched many people make their confessions. He felt their sincerity in the way they talked and the way they looked. They acted like children before a parent, admitting something they had done was wrong. Sills knew how hard it was for Ted to allow himself to be so vulnerable. *Especially hard for someone who's coming to confess he murdered someone*, Sills thought. *Had my embedded command technique worked? Had it nagged at Ted's subconscious throughout the weekend until he felt he had to unload the heavy burden of guilt?*

"Would you like a coke? Something else?" Sills asked.

"No thanks, I'm ready."

Sills started the tape recorder. "For the record, this is a conversation with Detective Benjamin Sills initiated solely by Ted Lapoltsky. Mr. Lapoltsky was informed that he has the right to remain silent and the right to an attorney. This statement is being recorded with his consent at 8:21 A.M on Sunday, February 15, 1998."

With a clear voice, Ted repeated all he had told Judge Boyd. When Ted said Elliot was the real killer, Sills thought he was cleverly trying to put the blame back on Elliot. But as the story unfolded, he knew in his gut that Ted was speaking the truth.

"This is too much for one week," Sills said, shaking his head in amazement. "I'll have the statement typed up for your signature. Let me know if there is any change you want to make. I don't know how I'll proceed. There are people I need to consult. This is a complicated story."

Sills almost felt sorry for Ted. He knew that he had to face the consequences of his actions. He had already paid a heavy price, losing his pride and probably his wife. "Both you and Elliot had visited the victim's apartment that night," Sills said. "No wonder this case was so confusing. I wonder how your confession is going to affect the outcome of Elliot's trial."

"We'll wait until tomorrow to see what Judge Boyd chooses to do," Ted said. "I'm out of that court case, that's for sure."

33

On Sunday morning, Saul Bernstein was finally located at his weekend retreat. He flew to New York, responding to Mr. Barrett's urgent request to represent Elliot. The lawyer was tall and slim. His gray hair was slicked back neatly. He was in his early sixties, with an aristocratic look and mannerisms. When he arrived at Elliot's house, Mr. Bernstein was greeted warmly by his friend.

Mr. Bernstein explained that the motion for dismissal would only be a formality. He suggested suing Ted for improper representation. Mr. Barrett agreed with enthusiasm but Elliot refused to discuss this possibility.

Elliot's parents invited Mr. Bernstein to join them for dinner at the Plaza. They also asked Ruth and Elliot to join them, but Elliot declined, saying he was exhausted and preferred to spend the rest of the evening at home. The telephone had not stopped ringing since Friday. Family members and friends called to congratulate Elliot on his acquittal. Reporters called to request comments and interviews. Elliot declined their requests, but Mr. Bernstein promised he would prepare a statement by Monday morning.

Ruth had been elated all weekend. She spoke to her family in Texas, sharing the happy news; they congratulated her on providing the key to Elliot's freedom.

The Barretts and Mr. Bernstein left for dinner. Ruth and Elliot were alone at home.

Ruth disconnected the phone, deciding she did not want to be disturbed. She stood in front of the wine rack, carefully choosing a bottle of good white wine, and carried it into the family room where Elliot was watching television. She opened the bottle, filled two glasses and shouted with glee. "It's all over! We are free!"

Elliot nodded, still feeling shocked. He smiled when he took the glass of wine from Ruth.

"After Monday, we will get our lives back," Ruth said with deep feeling.

"Yes, we will get our lives back," he repeated, not wanting to get into a lengthy conversation.

"How do you feel about all this? Will you ever talk about it? Now, what do you think about Ted?" Ruth asked, sensing his lack of enthusiasm.

Elliot got up and selected a video. "Let's just watch a movie, drink some wine and relax."

Ruth's disappointment spread over her face. "Come on. I want to talk to you. I'm bursting…"

"Fine. Speak if you want to. I'll listen."

"Forget it," she said, placing her glass dramatically on the table. "I thought we could finally have a conversation, but if that's the way you feel, I'm going to bed." She jumped up, making a point of displaying her anger, and walked toward the bedroom, hoping he would call her back. He didn't.

Ruth, feeling hurt, thought of turning around and confronting Elliot, but she decided to wait until tomorrow, after the dismissal of his case. Then, she would finally speak her mind and tell him everything she had been accumulating and holding inside for the past few months. *I do not always have to consider his feelings. I just wish he would consider me also. He is used to the idea that I'm here to support him. Things are going to be different from now on. I should stop being there for everyone else. It's time for me to consider myself too.*

Elliot sat motionless, staring blankly at the screen, feeling numb. He wanted to call Ruth back. He wanted to thank her for

her efforts and understanding during the trial, especially her helping him to gain his freedom, but he didn't do so. He could not face
her honest, loyal eyes. He still could not tell her that he had an
affair with Lindsey, that he had murdered Lindsey in a moment of
rage and insanity. She was so angry at what Ted tried to do to him,
but now Ted was going to jail for Elliot's crime.

For one brief moment, he contemplated going to Sills to confess everything and get out of this tormenting hell, but he knew
he would never do so. He felt the shame of his weakness and cow-
ardice. Elliot sunk deeper in the couch, flipping channels with the
remote control, not watching anything in particular. Finally he got
up and went to bed.

Early Monday morning Elliot's parent's arrived, excited, in a
hurry to get to the courthouse. That afternoon, they planned to fly
back to Boston. Ruth acted jubilant, not wanting Elliot's parents to
notice her anger. Nobody wanted to eat more than coffee and toast,
anxious to be on their way to the courthouse.

Mr. Bernstein gave them a quick briefing about what would be
happening that morning.

"All rise," the court clerk announced. This time Ruth was glad
to respond to the call. Judge Boyd entered the courtroom. She
looked at the jubilant faces of Ruth and Elliot's parents, feeling
sorry for what they would have to endure in such a short time.

Mr. Bernstein expected the procedure to last only a few minutes.
In a dry laconic voice he called for dismissal of the case. George
rose and, to their astonishment, said there was new evidence provided by Detective Sills that prevented dismissal. Mr. Bernstein was
shocked and demanded clarification.

Ruth's blood rushed to her head, feeling she was going to faint.
She could barely hear the rough explanation of the new findings.
Mr. Bernstein collected himself and tried to argue that after what
had happened Friday morning, dismissal was the only legal course
of action. Another person had been arrested in the case. George
argued that the jury verdict had already been rendered, and the

jury was ready to announce their verdict. Mr. Bernstein argued the danger of contamination was highly probable. Judge Boyd agreed with Bernstein's argument that Ted had not represented his client in good faith. She called for a recess until the next morning to allow time to search for precedents and prepare what could be a complicated ruling.

Elliot sat like a broken man, holding his head in his hands. Ruth felt as if she had no energy left in her body. "This is a nightmare," she said. Elliot's parents, profoundly confused, stood close to Mr. Bernstein, asking questions. George left the courtroom disappointed. *All these hours of hard work went down the drain!* He regretted having to conduct a new trial.

The news spread like fire in a dry field. Mr. Bernstein spoke to reporters, basically saying that he needed to learn more about the new allegations. He was already trying to rally the press in favor of Elliot, implying that the confusion in the district attorney's office was the worst he had ever experienced. He blamed the police for trying to obtain conviction at all costs, even going so far as to accuse an innocent man. He would demand dismissal of the case against Elliot.

Elliot's parents and Ruth and Elliot managed to leave through a back door and drive home. A large flock of reporters and television cameras waited their arrival at the gate of their house. The reporters surrounded the family and would not let them pass, demanding a response to their questions. The family refused to speak to the reporters and had to fight their way through the gate. A microphone hit Mr. Barrett in the face. He put his hand on the wound and felt blood running down his cheek. Mrs. Barrett started yelling hysterically. Angrily, Mr. Barrett pushed a reporter, who stumbled into a camera man. He lost his balance and dropped his camera on the concrete driveway, and it broke into pieces. Two reporters helped the camera man to his feet. Mr. Barratt managed to close the gate and heard the angry camera man yell that he would sue for damages.

34

Inside their home, all members of the family turned toward Elliot and demanded to know what was going on. Ruth knew that Elliot had not told the truth in quite a while. She demanded he confess whatever he knew to be true. Elliot couldn't take it any longer. Stifling a loud cry, he turned his back on them, stalked off, and locked himself in his bedroom. His father pounded on the door, but Elliot did not respond to any of his demands. Alone, he was reliving the night that had changed his life forever.

On that dreadful night of the twenty-eighth of September, after Lindsey regained consciousness, she called him at 9:20 P.M. She didn't like calling him at home, but took her usual precautions when calling a married man. She used her gallery phone and called his beeper.

Elliot was surprised and angry at Lindsey for calling him at home and at such a late hour. This relationship had gone too far. Their sex had been getting kinkier and seemed to increase in its intensity and risk, which frightened him. At their last encounter, Lindsey had tied him naked to the bed, gaining a promise that she could do anything she wanted. She explained that it was a test that demanded his complete trust in her. Reluctant, yet curious, Elliot had agreed to her request.

Lindsey picked up a razor, and to Elliot's horror, she started to press its sharp edge lightly on his skin. He was terrified of the possibility that she would leave a mark that would be impossible to explain to Ruth. Pictures of himself using a knife in the operating room popped into to his mind. He pleaded with her to stop, but Lindsey continued her game, teasing him and slowly moving her play to his groin. Amazingly, the fear intensified his pleasure. Using her mouth and her tongue she stimulated him while continuing to press the razor against his skin. Elliot felt his rising climax and the most intense mix of fear and pleasure he had ever experienced. The release left his body shaken, drained and utterly satisfied.

When it was all over, Elliot realized that he couldn't trust Lindsey, and he couldn't trust himself. He knew she had the audacity to venture into daring games that seemed increasingly too far for his endurance. He found himself caught between ending the relationship and succumbing to a new demanding, dark side of himself. Like an addict he wanted to experience more and more heightened pleasure.

Lindsey's call sealed Elliot's decision to call off their relationship. She had become too much of a risk.

"Hello," said Lindsey when he called back. "I'm sorry to call you at home, but something urgent has come up. I must talk to you immediately."

"It's too late tonight, I can't leave my house," Elliot said quietly.

"Say that you're needed at the hospital for an emergency."

Elliot wanted to end their relationship right there on the phone but he didn't want to embarrass her in such a cowardly way.

"I'll be there in twenty minutes," he said.

Ruth was asleep. He got into his car and drove to SoHo. Lindsey opened the door with an inviting smile, looking beautiful in a simple dress. For a moment he wanted to forget his resolve to end their affair. She hugged him tight and gave him a deep, passionate kiss. "I'm so happy you came."

"Something about you is different tonight. What is it? You seem so emotional," Elliot asked as they went upstairs to her living room.

"I had a rough night. I just finished a relationship."

Elliot knew she was talking about another man. "That doesn't seem like something that would stir such emotions in you. You said you don't get attached."

"Usually, I can handle anything. But tonight I feel vulnerable, and I wanted you at my side. I feel secure with you."

Elliot knew that this was the wrong time to end his relationship with Lindsey. He could tell that she wanted passion and possession tonight, but he could not give her what she wanted. *I must stop seeing her,* he decided. Elliot hesitated for a moment, considering how to approach this. "Lindsey. Listen. We've had a great time. Probably my most passionate time ever. But we should stop seeing each other."

"I only want to be with you tonight," Lindsey said kissing his neck and ear.

Elliot shook her away. Her demands and enticements always pulled him deeper. In her own way, she asked more of him than he wanted to give. "I'm sorry. I have to go."

"What are you saying?" Lindsey was astounded. The two men she was involved with were taking control away from her. That was too much for one night. "Do you think it's just that easy?" she said coldly.

"What are you saying? We both understood this could end at any time."

"I don't care that you're married. I don't care that you see me only when it's convenient."

"Please. Don't make it harder than it already is. But I can't keep on. I just can't…"

Lindsey's eyes grew narrow, and her temper was ready to burst. "Do you think you control this? You don't."

Elliot didn't like her threatening tone. He knew she could make trouble for him. He was unable to think of a more effective approach to use with her.

"I haven't said this to any man before. I have fallen in love with you," Lindsey said softly, trying again to seduce Elliot. She started running her tongue along his neck.

Elliot recognized her words as a ploy: Lindsey did not love, she controlled. "This relationship was never about love, and you know that. I love my wife."

"I don't need you to leave your family. I'm a grown and inde-pendent woman," she said, trying to persuade him.

"Please be reasonable. It's getting too late. I must leave."

"No..."

"Listen to me. I don't want to be with you anymore. I can't make it clearer than that."

Lindsey stepped closer, furious, and threatened to expose their relationship. Elliot angrily said she could do as she liked, but he was leaving.

Lindsey was outraged. "Leaving?" she shouted. "How about a little scandal for a going-away present? I could scream at the top of my lungs. The police would come. Would your sweet wife enjoy being married to a rapist?"

Enraged at Lindsey's cunning and the ugliness of her threat, he looked at her with hatred. She laughed at him. She stood up and moved again toward him, trying to grab his hand. She slowly opened her mouth and pretended to scream.

Elliot pushed her down on the couch. "Stop it," he said des-perately, as he tried to leave. Suddenly, Lindsey let out a pierc-ing scream. Frantically, Elliot turned back, pushed her and held her hands above her head, trying to stop her attempt to grab and scratch his face. She tried to get free of his tight hold with her hands. Elliot pressed his body over hers. With one hand he pushed her hands under her body while grabbing the pillow to shove over her face. He just wanted to quiet her. Elliot's mind blanked; time stopped. When she stopped moving and struggling, and her body went limp, he realized the horrid reality that he had gone too far.

The banging on the door woke Elliot from his trance. The blow of facing himself with the knowledge that he had killed Lindsey struck with its full strength. Pain knifed his chest. "I killed a human being," he said. The full implication of his madness paralyzed him with terror. For a swift second, he contemplated the sweetness of ending the humiliating pain and agony by committing suicide, but knew he could not carry it through.

With his last strength, Elliot opened the door and stood ashamed before his family, knowing that the inevitable journey for truth must play out its course.

EPILOGUE

Judge Boyd ruled for a new trial with a new jury. Elliot was convicted of second degree murder and received the maximum sentence of ten years.

The Supreme Court ruled in Ted's case that a man's right to defend himself supersedes attorney-client privilege.

Ted was disbarred but he was allowed to teach law and did so for many years.

Heather returned to Ted. They went to a marriage counselor and had a child through in-vitro fertilization. Judge Boyd agreed to be the godmother.

Ruth divorced Elliot and went back to live in Texas. She settled near Austin and began raising horses.

George became a state Supreme Court judge.

Ted wisely never charged Elliot for his services.

DAVID PINTO was born in Israel and has lived in the United States for over 40 years. He studied at the University of Michigan and the University of Texas, graduating with a degree in architecture from U-T. He designs and builds large residential homes in Austin Texas.

9 781942 762546